A PACKET OF TROUBLE

When Jake agreed to take Gostoli's packet to Austria it had been "for kicks" as much as for the money. He'd been warned to expect trouble so it was no surprise when the bandy-legged Grogan came muscling-in, but when Hudson and Poxy burst in on the scene and the bullets began to fly, he wondered if he'd been an idiot. . . .

Then there was Nella—a passionate capricious Nella! Where did she fit in and why did she pack a gun?

This is the action-packed story of Jake Standish's exciting struggle to reach Innsbruck, of moments of triumph and disaster. There is suspense, violence and romance here. The reader is slammed straight into top gear and raced forward until he reaches the unexpected climax.

A PACKET
OF TROUBLE

by

F. U. ASHFORD

ROBERT HALE & COMPANY
63 Old Brompton Road, London S.W.7

© *F. U. Ashford 1971*
First published in Great Britain 1971

ISBN 0 7091 1782 5

Printed in Great Britain by A. Wheaton & Co., Exeter

To Eileen

MINUS ONE

It HAD been easy, like going through a piece of cheese. A good hard thump, and the knife was in; up to the hilt. He felt the old man go limp against him and slump to the floor. How frail he looked! By the pencil of light from the torch he gazed at the pale, heavily lined face, at the dead-white hair, the staring eyes, the scrawny neck. "Poor devil," he murmured, turning the body over.

Kneeling now, he grasped the knife in his gloved hand, and pulled. . . . It was as easy coming out as going in. He cleaned it on the old man's cardigan, away from the growing splodge of crimson.

What was it they'd said? "No violence, unless absolutely necessary."

He sighed. If the old man had not come down—caught him in the act—seen his face. . . .

"Best get out of here, and quick. . . ."

He crossed to the table—again that pencil of light—and there, by the side of the table-lamp, was the box. Lifting the cover, he glanced inside, and his features relaxed into a smile of satisfaction. Quickly he replaced the cover and slipped the tiny box into his pocket.

"Now," he muttered, "deliver the goods and collect. . . ."

He turned the beam of light to the floor as he crossed the room. Already, on the bare boards, a trickle of red had become a pool.

Meanwhile, in a house in Maida Vale, two men waited.

"We should have heard by now, Andre," said the taller.

Pulling nervously at his cigarette, he went on, "Hope to God nothing's gone wrong."

Andre—obese and oily—removed his thick-lensed glasses and rubbed them vigorously. "Calm yourself, Caleb, calm yourself. Everything will be all right."

The bearded Caleb shook his head. "I don't like it."

The minutes ticked by. The silence became oppressive. Suddenly Caleb got up and paced the room. "And what if there's violence? What if he rubs him out? I'm asking you —where will we be then? What will happen to us?"

"Keep calm," replied Andre blandly, smoothing his double chin with a podgy hand. "No one knows about us. Besides, Bobo's a professional. He's well paid, and if anything goes wrong he'll take his medicine. Bobo won't talk."

"And if he gets the . . . the thing, how are we going to get rid of it? Well never get it to . . ."

"Shut up, you fool," shouted Andre, drowning him. "Control yourself, man, for God's sake." Then, the bland smile returning, he continued, "There's nothing to worry about— absolutely nothing. My plans are laid; there will be no hitch. It will be delivered."

At his elbow the telephone rang, cutting short further conversation. Andre reached out a hand. For a moment he listened, while the smile faded from his face.

"I see," he said quietly. Then replaced the receiver.

"Well?"

"The old man's dead," replied Andre.

Bachelor, 27, good physique, needs £2,000.
Will tackle anything legal. (Box 009B.)
—Extract from a London newspaper.

ONE

GOSTOLI seized Jake's hand in a sticky, two-fisted grip, and with a smile—sleek and soapy—hustled him into a chair. Glancing furtively towards the door of the outer office, he crossed the room, the bare boards creaking beneath his weight.

"It would never do to be overheard," he said, turning the key.

"I suppose not," replied Jake dubiously, glancing about him.

Jacob Standish, 'Jake' to his friends, was disappointed. He'd expected something more plush. On the door as he came in he'd seen the words 'ANDRE GOSTOLI. DEALER'. He doubted if Gostoli's dealings brought much profit. The flaking paintwork; the execrable furniture and fittings! And the approach—five floors up! Little hope of getting £2,000 here: the place screamed penury.

"So my premises don't impress you, Mr Standish," said Gostoli. "Appearances are sometimes deceptive, you know . . . and if it's the money you're worrying about . . ."

"I just wondered."

Gostoli sat down opposite Jake, peering at him. Already his quick perception had decided him. He'd noted the florid complexion, the dark unruly hair, the determined chin, and the dark audacious eyes. This is our man, he thought. Aloud, he said, "Mr Standish. This money . . . this two thousand. It is—how you say—chicken fodder? You do your work well . . . I pay."

"What work? You've told me nothing yet."

"I will tell you." It was a curious accent—Continental, of course. Strange name, too.

Gostoli began talking. Told him he was a dealer in stamps. This much was obvious from the framed sets on the walls and the albums on the surrounding shelves. The desk, too, was littered with the impedimenta of his trade—even a copy of the *Philatelic Weekly*. Following Jake's eyes, he opened it at a page. "There." He pointed a podgy finger. "That's one of my advertisements."

Then the questions began. Where did Jake go to school? What did he do for a living? What was his father?

"I didn't come here for an inquisition."

"You cannot expect to be taken on trust . . . blindly. . . . I must ask questions," replied Gostoli soothingly.

"Oh, all right." Stifling a smile, Jake added, "We have to trust each other, anyway."

"Well, I trust you now, Mr Standish." Gostoli's face beamed.

"Let's get on with it, then."

Gradually Gostoli unfolded his story. "Yes," his voice rose as he warmed to his subject. "But you must not ask me how this great rarity came into my possession. I can tell you, though, that the British Guiana 4 cents of 1856—a fabulous stamp—is worth many thousands." He opened a book at his side. "See," he cried, pointing to a coloured plate, "there it is. Isn't it wonderful?"

"What? A piece of blue paper like that?"

"Of course . . . and unobtainable at that. But this rarity of mine . . . this is something undreamed of. It is what we in the trade call 'an error'. You see," he went on, pointing again to the coloured plate, "somehow the 'U' and the 'I' got transposed. On my stamp the word 'GUIANA' is printed 'GIUANA'. Mr Standish . . . it is priceless. Naturally it was important to keep its existence a secret, anyway for a time, but unfortunately the information leaked out. You really must understand the magnitude of this rarity. It is quite unprecedented . . . *it is worth a fortune.* Already some rogues have made an unsuccessful attempt to rob me of it. So far I have been lucky. But these men are dangerous—they will stop at nothing."

"Interesting," mused Jake. "Where do I come in?"

"Good question—good question," returned Gostoli, rubbing his hands excitedly. "You see," he continued, "I have been fortunate to place this great rarity with a private collector on the Continent. The price is handsome. I want you, Mr Standish—Jacob—to take it there for me."

Jake ignored the slimy cordiality. At least they were getting somewhere. "These men?" he asked. "You say they'd stop at nothing. Killers . . . you mean?"

"Certainly. But that you must not permit. I want the stamp delivered."

The coolness of it! He let it pass. "It's a tall order."

"Think of the money," continued Gostoli. "I must not go. They would follow . . . steal my treasure . . . perhaps even do away with me. But you," a cunning smile creased his podgy face, "they do not know. You will be safe."

A slippery one! thought Jake. Still . . . if he got most of the money in advance it could be worth-while. Not that the money was everything. The thing was to get away from monotony. . . . God—how bored can you get? . . . He'd always been the same, bored unless rampaging about. He smiled, remembering his schooldays: that final year at Attenborra's 'a place where boys are permitted freedom of expression', as it was described. Even so, there came the time when he and his friend Nicco Bullivant expressed themselves too freely, even for Attenborra's. They'd been great friends, these two, inseparable, yet after that they'd drifted apart. He hadn't seen Nicco for years now. The last he heard was that he was married and living in Germany. Pity! He was a grand chap.

"You'll do it?" Gostoli's eager voice jolted him back. He hesitated.

Gostoli pressed on hurriedly. "No one will suspect you.

Listen. I will put a thousand pounds . . . cash . . . into your bank tomorrow. The other thousand on delivery. What you say?"

"Expenses?"

"Naturally."

It was a good offer. Bound to be excitement. . . . Pity Nicco wasn't around. Obviously the money would be useful, though he got by well enough. He had a sudden thought. "It's all above board, I suppose? Legal, you know?"

"Quite."

"What about the Customs?"

"Ah, that!" Gostoli blinked. "You'd be obliged to run the Customs."

"Smuggling? You call that legal?"

"It's done every day. You'll find it easy."

"Why not just send the thing by post? Registered."

"What?" The voice rose to a scream. "It would be confiscated."

"I said I'd tackle anything legal. It's not what I call legal."

"Do not worry . . . Jacob. Rest assured that once the stamp is delivered I'll square the Customs. What is called . . . invisible exports."

Obviously, Gostoli was lying. Jake pondered a moment, taking in the forced smile. It wasn't that the Customs worried him unduly : it added to the thrill. If only Nicco were around; just up his street. They'd get the stamp through. Funny he kept thinking about Nicco. Suddenly his mind was made up.

"All right, Gostoli," he said. "I'll do it."

It was more than an hour before they separated. There was still much to discuss. There must be no hitch; every detail had to be considered. Gostoli was delighted at Jake being an artist. "Couldn't be better," he enthused. "Put your painting things in your car, and be perfectly natural : an artist on holiday painting landscapes. No one will suspect you. It is . . . just perfect." Finally he told Jake in a whisper that he was to go to Innsbruck.

There was another hot, two-fisted grip when he got up to go. "The cash and the packet will be at your bank tomorrow," said Gostoli. "Get your passage booked, then—how you say?—scram! One last word—remember, the packet will be sealed. This must not be broken : otherwise the buyer will not pay. And remember, too, we must not meet again before you go, and on no account get in touch with me. Good luck."

It was raining hard and almost dark when Jake reached his room in West Kensington. Once a meeting-house of some sort, it now served as his bedroom, studio and kitchen. He closed the door, hurried across the sparsely furnished room and closed the skylight through which the rain was beating. He moved over to a stove and, knocking out his pipe, flung himself into an armchair. He smiled happily. At last—boredom was gone. Now perhaps he would get to grips with something stimulating, dangerous even : to say nothing of the cash! He began to plan. Should he take the old Hillman, or should he hire? Passport? That was in force, anyway. . . . The soliloquy ended abruptly when the door opened and a man—a complete stranger—walked in.

"Sorry, old chap." He was middle-aged and well dressed. His fashionable beard suited him. "My name's Prescott. I did knock," he explained, "but you couldn't have heard."

"That's O.K. Come on in."

The stranger held out his hand. He glanced towards the door. "Can't be overheard, I suppose?" he asked.

"Not a chance. Anyway, why the mystery?"

"Hush!" urged Prescott. He lowered his voice. "I've come from Gostoli."

It was so unexpected that for a moment Jake was at a loss. But Prescott's next words reassured him. "Gostoli said you'd understand if I mentioned British Guiana."

"But . . . this is ridiculous. . . ."

"Listen. There's been a hitch . . . all plans are changed. He must see you immediately."

"I was told, on no account . . ."

"I know. But there's no alternative. What's happened is serious. You must come . . . without delay."

"Very well."

Outside, a van was drawn up against the pavement. Rain was still sheeting down. What a night for mid-May!

"Better run for it," urged Prescott. They reached the back of the van and scrambled inside. Then the driver slammed in the clutch.

A partition between the rear of the van and the driver's compartment, and the obscured windows, made it impossible for Jake to see where he was going. Prescott seemed strangely quiet, and any attempt to engage him in conversation was a dead loss. Once, asking him where they were going, all he got was a taciturn "It's better you not know." Two or three times he tried to peer out of the rear windows. Eventually this brought a sulky "Give over—you won't see anything: they're whitewashed."

Before Jake could reply, the van swerved and, with a screech of brakes, jerked to a standstill.

"Here we are," announced Prescott.

As they alighted, Jake saw they were in a dimly-lit mews, surrounded by high walls. Then the driver—a wizened little fellow—came round and caught him by the arm, urging him forward. A runt of a man, this—Jake pushed him roughly away.

"Hurry," said the driver.

Hustling him through a door, they led him up some stairs and into an uncarpeted room lit by a single fly-blown electric bulb. The only furniture was a deal table with a chair on either side. This was not the room where he'd talked to Gostoli earlier! A feeling of unease came over him—the darkened van—the mystery of their whereabouts—the haste —and now the strange room!

"Where's Gostoli?" he flung, suspicion aroused.

"Calm yourself, Mr Standish . . . all is well."

Prescott crossed to the table and lowered himself into a

chair. "There are some papers here . . ." As he spoke he opened a drawer in front of him. The next instant an automatic was in his hand.

"No tricks, Mr S.," he commanded, covering him. "The man behind the gun always wins."

So they'd fooled him! The blood surged to his head, and in his anger he would have rushed forward, but something hard shoved against his back checked him. "Don't do anything you'll regret," said the runty driver. "I'm a handy marksman."

Toying with the automatic, Prescott was talking again. "Sorry about Gostoli," he said. "Fact is, we can't produce him . . . don't know him even. We've been obliged to—shall we say?—invite you here to answer some questions."

"You'll be lucky. . . ."

"Don't interrupt. As I said, we have some questions to ask . . . and a proposition to make. If you behave, you'll not get hurt. Otherwise . . ." He raised a finger to his head and clicked his tongue.

"Bastard!"

The ease with which they'd tricked him—it hurt; humiliated him. Of all the idiots. Well, Gostoli had saved his money, anyway.

Prescott continued. "We know Gostoli's hired you as a carrier . . . no use denying it. Now, you tell us . . . where you're going . . . and why."

"Oh, belt up."

"You'll talk presently. We have ways. . . ."

"I have nothing to say," replied Jake. Already humiliation was giving way to defiance. How the hell had they got on to him so quickly? Prescott, too? He hadn't looked a rogue. Well, he'd be damned if they'd get away with it. If they wanted information, let 'em fight for it. He began to think of ways. . . .

"You're going east, we know that." Prescott smiled. "Might it be . . . Innsbruck, perhaps?"

Cautiously, every time the man's eyes were not directly

upon him, Jake was probing his surroundings. He noticed the door beyond the table. Perhaps, with a rush?

"If you know, or think you know, why ask?"

"Could it be you're to carry something valuable . . . a stamp, for instance?"

Jake yawned.

"So it's to be a thousand down, is it, and another thousand on delivery?" continued Prescott imperturbably.

It was impossible to hide surprise. They knew everything.

"Ah!" There was triumph in his voice. "You see, Mr S., we know it all. So now, perhaps, you'll listen and, maybe, you'll change your mind and *come in with us*. We're prepared to be generous. We'll give you a couple of thousand to pass the packet over to us."

So that was it. A double-cross. Jake said nothing, and Prescott went on, "You can take Gostoli's thousand . . . go to the Continent, and come back later saying you've been robbed. Dead easy . . . three thousand instead of two—and no risk.

So he was useful to them alive, was he? That simplified matters : until he got the packet they'd not shoot. He would wait his chance, then put to good use that six months' workout he'd recently done in King's gymnasium.

"A couple of thousand?" he echoed, playing for time.

"Yes . . . you going to be sensible?" The question came eagerly enough, yet it lacked conviction.

The moment came, almost before he was ready. The pressure in the small of his back eased. Instinctively he knew the driver had lowered his gun. With a gesture of supposed horror, Jake pointed to the door. "No, no," he screamed. Prescott whipped round, his face enigmatic. Instantly Jake dropped to his knees, and with one of King's favourite moves rolled himself over and came up behind the driver. The gun dropped to the floor noisily—it was only Prescott now! But Prescott, rigid in his chair, seemed paralysed. Jake's blood was racing : there was to be no let-up. He seized the driver by the collar and seat of his trousers. "Come on, you runt," he cried. "See how you like the real thing." Lifting him bodily, he flung him at the gaping Prescott. He landed heavily across the table and slid limply to the floor, taking Prescott with him. Jake was taking no chances; he grabbed a chair and swung it aloft to make an end of it. At that instant he heard footsteps. Someone was thumping up the stairs, shouting. As the door burst open he whipped round, and with all his strength flung the chair. It took the man full on the chest, and with a sigh he fell to the floor. In the sudden hush, realisation came to Jake.

The man was Gostoli!

TWO

THE day was fine for the Channel crossing. Jake looked at his watch. He was always restless and wanting to be on the move.

He thought of Gostoli, his mind drifting back 72 hours to when he'd nearly finished him off. If the man hadn't played such a damn fool trick he wouldn't have got hurt. Thought he was being clever. Called it 'an honesty test', wanted to prove Jake was to be trusted, or whether he'd succumb to bribery. His colleague, Caleb Prescott, had suggested it. Still, they'd proved their point—knew now he was O.K. It amused Jake, remembering Gostoli's insistence that they should not meet again. They'd met all right . . . been around together most of that night. Been to 'Casualty' at two hospitals before getting attention.

It was almost daylight when Prescott drove him back to the studio. Before leaving, he asked Jake for one of his shoes.

"Good God, whatever for?"

"The Customs, of course," said Prescott. "Give me a shoe and we'll have it fixed so you can carry the packet inside the heel. It's been done many times, but you'll be all right." Prescott explained how the heel worked. "We'll send it to the bank with the packet."

Gostoli kept his word. Jake had called at the bank, got the parcels and confirmed that the cash was in his account. Back in his studio, he'd transferred the packet to the hollow heel. It worked perfectly, and he was amazed at the ease with which he could snap it into position. There had been no difficulty with the Customs at Dover. The man had asked the usual questions, and taken only a fleeting glance into the Hillman. Then he'd waved him on.

Jake crossed to the deserted side of the boat. No sign of the Belgian coastline yet—too soon, anyway. Try a drink, he thought.

At the bar a heated argument was going on between a passenger and the white-coated barman. The passenger, chewing a cigar end, was a short, thick-set man in a dark suit and a black slouch hat.

"And I tell you," his high treble voice was raised, "that a gin and dubonnet should be a shilling cheaper."

Jake had never seen a man more grotesque: the enormous breadth of shoulder, the long arms and the short, bandy legs. A gorilla of a man, with the voice of a pip-squeak!

"Well," replied the barman with a shrug, "that's the price you pay here."

Exasperated, the black-hatted man slammed his glass back on the counter. "Very well," he spluttered shrilly, "you can keep the bloody stuff." As he turned, his eyes met Jake's, and he gave a noticeable start of surprise. Then, pulling hard at his cigar, he hurried away down the saloon with the rolling gait peculiar to the bandy-legged.

"No satisfying some people," grumbled the barman as he mixed Jake's drink. "Not like other men, I'd say—with those shoulders and the voice of a choir-boy."

Jake took the drink to a table. He wanted to think . . . This odd fellow in the black hat . . . the strange look he'd given him. Was it one of recognition? He couldn't place the man. Looked like a bruiser—somebody's sparring partner— yet, that voice! Could it be one of the crowd Gostoli had warned him against? Nonsense! If he were going to start imagining stuff like this already . . .

An hour later he drove the Hillman away from the Customs shed and out into the sunshine. The A.A. and the Customs had been perfect gentlemen: there was absolutely nothing to it. They hadn't even asked questions. He tapped the bogus heel on the floor of the car, and smiled. No longer had he to bother about failing at the first fence, anyway.

A few hundred yards from the Customs shed he stopped and parked by a low wall. So this was Ostend! In the bright sunshine it was a gay scene, one which fired his imagination. What was it Gostoli had said? "Take it leisurely—be an artist on holiday." On the boat he had toyed with the idea of spending the first night at Bruges. It was only twenty-five kilometres off : plenty of time to knock out a water-colour!

Near the quay he found a green-shuttered café. Over a snack and a half-bottle of *Chateauneuf* he dallied pleasantly for an hour. Then he went back to his car to collect his painting gear.

His easel set up, it was only a matter of minutes before he had completed the faint outline of the pencil work. Picking up his paint-box, he began to mix the blue for the first wash —the sky. Pure cobalt, this. . . . He paused a moment to look again at the drawing. Something about the curve of the quay did not satisfy him. Holding his pencil at arm's length, he moved it about, checking his proportions. He stopped suddenly. . . . It wasn't as if he minded being watched when he was painting—but this was different : the man was twenty yards away. Partially hidden behind a fish stall, the fellow was standing motionless, gazing fixedly at him. In his dark clothes and black slouch hat, so at variance with the colour around him, there could be no doubt!

Jake paused, lowered his pencil, and with dead-pan expression, stared back. Their eyes met, and at once the man slipped behind the stall. A moment later Jake picked out the black-hatted figure further along the quay. There was no mistaking the massive shoulders and those hurrying bandy legs.

THREE

THE hotel seemed comfortable enough. Perhaps, as an artist, a more aesthetic view from the window would have been preferable. No one could conjure any charm from the cobbled courtyard below, bounded on one side by lock-up garages, and on the other by the kitchen quarters and an overgrown shrubbery. Now, his suitcase emptied and his few clothes put away, Jake stood by the window contemplating this uninspiring scene. Dinner did not begin until 8 o'clock. Better have a look at the town.

A walk of a few minutes down the narrow street brought him out into the busy *Markt*. Here, dominating its surroundings, the great tri-sectioned Belfry was already casting an elongated shadow. Skirting the Market Place, he turned into a street rich in medieval buildings, and presently came to a canal. This was the real Bruges! A place where an artist could lose himself. For an hour he roamed the canals, past ancient stone bridges and beneath friendly walls. Presently a setting, transcending anything he'd yet seen, caught his eye. He crossed to an iron seat built round the base of a large tree, and sat down to gaze on the scene. How cool and peaceful here upon the seat, his back resting against the tree trunk. With so much beauty around him, time stood still.

"One thing at a time. . . ."

Just five words from the other side of the tree, but they hit Jake as a blow in the stomach. Surely there could be only one voice quite like this. . . .

Another voice now, low and petulant. "Now, Grogan,"

the words came slowly. "Why the secrecy? Why get me from Antwerp so fast?"

"Because we're after something . . . a knock-out! That's why." The reply, high-pitched, effeminate, left no room for doubt.

"A knockout, eh?"

"Yep. An' no bigger'n a match-box."

Jake froze, every muscle taut. This was no coincidence. It must be . . .

"Another couple of days in Antwerp and I'd have had 'em—diamonds!"

"Nothing to do with me, Chesney," whined Grogan. "Larry has spoke, and when Larry speaks, we act. This'll be better'n a few diamonds, anyway . . . and we'll get our cut."

"Well, if Larry says so." The man called Chesney sounded appeased.

"He said you was to be roped in. That we must tail the bloke and get the stuff. . . . Pronto, before someone else gets there."

"What's the loot, then?" asked Chesney.

"Dunno. But Larry wants it—wants it bad . . . sell to the highest bidder an' all that."

A whiff of cigar smoke drifted across, stale and pungent. Then—"Kid gloves?" asked Chesney.

"Not bleeding likely. If he's difficult, says Larry, cosh 'im."

Chesney laughed—a sinister laugh. "Cor," he breathed, "an' a cosh from Groge is something. Remember in Liverpool . . . split his head like a duck egg."

Listening, Jack knew it was time he moved. Must get away without being followed. A dozen questions were yet to be answered—Did they know here he was staying? What was their plan? When would they strike, and where? But he mustn't stay—might lose the advantage he'd gained.

He looked around for a way of escape. An impossible task! The moment he left the tree, they'd see him. But luck was with him. Bearing down on him, in the company of a guide, was a party of tourists. He did not hesitate. As they passed, jabbering excitedly, he stood up, and with a murmured "Thought I'd lost you all", tacked himself on to a young man with long hair. Nobody seemed surprised at his presence, and, feeling safer with every step, he chatted happily to his new companion. The party crossed a bridge and, turning into a deserted street, gathered round the guide. Jake unobtrusively detached himself and slipped away. The voice of the guide, monotonous and repetitive, faded into the distance, "We will soon be coming to the Beguinage. . . ."

Hurrying back to the bridge, Jake looked back along the canal. The two men were still on the seat, but as he watched they got up and began walking away. The man called Chesney, tall and erect, wore nondescript clothes, and Jake doubted if he would recognise him again. Not so Grogan, cigar in mouth, stumping along—bow legs unmistakable, familiar black hat well down on his ears.

Dinner at the hotel was a dull affair. The clientele, mostly English, had no place in Jake's thoughts. He was now fully aware that, despite Gostoli's assurances, these men—Grogan and Chesney—were on to him. The 'artist on holiday' image was a dead duck. Not that it worried him: he'd come into it for kicks. If only he could have stayed behind the tree longer: maybe he'd have heard all their plans. That they intended using violence went without saying, and if one of Grogan's coshings wasn't adequate they'd obviously use more effective measures. Jake sighed, wishing now he'd taken Gostoli's advice and armed himself.

A white-haired waiter came fussing over him, menu in hand. "Monsieur should try the *Bombe Flandre*."

"Eh?"

"Monsieur should try . . ."

"Oh! Sorry." Jake was jerked back to the present. "*Bombe Flandre*? What is it?"

"Marzipan, chocolate and nuts . . . with ice-cream. Delicious."

"All right. If you recommend it."

Left to himself, Jake returned to his problems. One thing

was certain. If they were smart enough to have followed him so far, they should have no difficulty in finding out where he was staying. The sensible thing, therefore, was to move; clear out now, without waiting for morning. The question was, where? So far he had made no plans beyond taking Bruges in the itinerary. Should he go to Brussels or try some less direct route? He thought of the A.A. Guide in his room. If he got it now, he could study the maps while having his coffee and cognac.

He passed the waiter on the way out. "Back in a moment," he threw at him.

Reaching the door of his room, he felt in his pocket for the key. He was putting it in the heyhole when it slipped from his grasp and clattered to the floor. "Damn." He stooped to retrieve it. . . .

What was that?

It came from within the room, sounding like the slam of a drawer. Could it be? His pulses racing, he rammed in the key and burst into the room.

It was empty.

At the open window a half-drawn curtain moved. He reached it in a flash and tore it aside. . . . No one there. He stood for a moment, nonplussed. Then a faint but unmistakable smell of cigar smoke caught his nostrils. He knew at once. Grogan was in the room—hiding! Glancing towards the bed, Jake smiled. It was old-fashioned : a man could lie beneath it. A brass candlestick on the mantelpiece caught his eye. He grabbed it.

"Come out Grogan," he cried. "I know you're there."

No reply. Taut, expectant, he waited, straining to hear the slightest movement. Across the square a clock began striking the hour, its tone deep and melodious. Somewhere a moped raced. Approaching the bed, he seized the bedding and mattress, and tore them aside. Nothing.

It was impossible—the man could not have escaped. Yet he'd been there. Jake sought another hiding place, but there was nowhere else. He went back to the window : the court-

yard was deserted. In any case, no man could have jumped
—the ground was fifteen feet below. He leaned out. Then
the truth hit him. Away to the left, no more than a yard
distant, and running from the top floor to the ground, was a
fire-escape. On each floor a metal platform connected to a
door in the hotel. A man—a short one even—could have
stepped from the platform to the window-sill of his room.

Leaning out, probing every corner of the empty yard
below, a feeling of frustration passed over him. If only he'd
not dropped the damned key. . . .

FOUR

GROGAN had been searching, of course. It stood out a mile
when Jake opened the chest of drawers. Though everything
in the bottom drawer had been turned out and shovelled
back regardless, the top drawer was untouched. He'd obviously interrupted the man before he'd completed his search.
The question now was, would Grogan return to finish the
job? Abstractedly, Jake fingered the packet, now attached to
a thin chain round his neck : better than the hollow heel,
which he felt had served its purpose. He was furious with
himself; he should have anticipated some such visit. One
thing was certain, anyway—he must leave the hotel. Clear
out now, and leave a false trail.

Crossing the room for his suitcase, he stopped suddenly.
Would men of this calibre let him get away with this?
They'd be watching the hotel. What happened now? There
was only one thing to do—find out.

The light was failing, so, crossing to the window, he drew
the curtains. Then, switching on the light, he began moving
about the room so that his shadow was visible from outside.
He whistled softly, relieved to be taking some positive action
and enjoying the subterfuge. His whereabouts must surely
now be obvious to any watcher. After a few minutes of this
he slipped out on to the landing, leaving the bedroom light
on. Keeping clear of the windows, he made for the lavatory.
Unobserved, he went in and locked the door behind him.
The little room was dark, and when he drew back the
curtain he looked down at the courtyard !

For several minutes he stood watching the rear gateway, his eyes straining to catch any movement in the gathering gloom. Presently he heard footsteps, and someone tried the handle. It was obvious he mustn't stay here too long. The minutes passed. Then, all at once, his patience was rewarded. A shadow, squat and broad, appeared at the side of the gateway—appeared and was gone. It was only momentary, illusionary almost, but there was something else. From the shadow came a fleeting glow, red and unmistakable. It was enough : Grogan was there. He flushed the lavatory and stepped out on to the landing.

Back in his room, he guessed Chesney would be watching the front entrance. Not that this made any difference, because he couldn't get his car out that way. He sat for a time on the edge of the bed, smoking and thinking, and presently the solution came to him. As a plan it was not perfect, but it ought to succeed. Grinning, he reached for his suitcase and began to pack.

Stars were already flickering in the clear night sky when he reached the shrubbery. A three-quarter moon bathed the scene in an incandescent light, throwing deep shadows across the cobbled yard. From his hiding-place Jake was able to see the rear gateway, the fire-escape and the lock-up where his car was housed. How long the vigil would last was anybody's guess. Peering through the undergrowth, he looked up to the window of the room he'd recently vacated. The light was out now; the curtains drawn, the window shut and latched.

What a tale he'd had to tell to explain his sudden departure. But his passage had been smoothed when he said he would pay the hotel's full charges. "It is necessary," he explained, "to evade someone who is proving an embarrassment to me. I will vacate my room during the night, and will leave the key in the door." As an afterthought, he left a phoney forwarding address : some hotel in Luxembourg where a friend had once stayed.

A few minutes before midnight he left his bedroom and crept down the back stairs. The kitchen, in darkness but for a shaft of moonlight from the window, led through to a narrow passage and to a door. Stealthily, he opened it a few inches and through the opening saw a tiny paved walk leading to an outbuilding. In front of him, a bare six feet off, was the shrubbery. To reach it, all he had to do was to cross the narrow space. Gripping the suitcase, he stepped outside, closing the door carefully behind him. The latch was old and slipped back into place with a sharp click. To his keyed-up nerves it was like the blare of a klaxon. Still as death, he held himself within the meagre porchway, listening. All was quiet. He braced himself and stepped out into the moonlight. Two paces, and he was in the shrubbery, safe. He breathed again, then step by step edged his way forward. Briars, rapier sharp, tore at his clothes, but at last he reached the spot where he must wait. Here, opposite the lock-up garages, he lowered his suitcase to the ground.

Slowly—minute by dragging minute—time passed. The clock in the distance chimed the quarters : the drone of an occasional car broke the silence. A droning, louder than the rest, reminded him of the reliance he was placing on the Hillman : there must be no show of temperament. If the old veteran did not start at once, he'd be done. He thought, too, of the split-second timing—utterly vital. The route as well. That, at least, was clued-up. The porter had said turn right into the lane, and when he reached the *Markt* to take the next right, then follow the sign to the motorway. Sounded easy enough.

Presently he began wondering. Had he let his imagination run riot? Was it really Grogan, that dim shape? More than once he fancied he heard a movement or caught a whiff of cigar. Imagination again. Time passed, one o'clock and—hours later—two o'clock. Surely he must come. Suddenly he stiffened. From the gateway came a faint sound. Instinctively he knew this was it. As he watched, a shadow appeared, and a moment later Grogan stepped into view. There was no mistaking him; the massive shoulders, the bandy legs !

Pulling his hat down so that his face was almost hidden,

Grogan glanced furtively about, then waddled into the court-yard. Passing close to where Jake stood, rigid and expectant, he took the cigar from his mouth and flung it towards the shrubbery. Then, with short silent footsteps, he crossed the yard and was lost to view. A moment later he reappeared, mounting the fire-escape. Something in his hand—a knife, perhaps—glinted as he climbed.

Everything now depended upon exact timing. Must give the man a second or two to start on the window, but not long enough to discover the room empty. Jake grasped the suit-case. He could see Grogan fiddling with the catch—it was a knife! Now. . . .

Brushing the foliage aside, Jake broke cover and raced towards the garage. His echoing footsteps sounded to him like cannon fire. He heard a muffled cry. Now he was by the lock-up. The key turned easily and the door swung open. Two seconds later he was in the car, with the ignition on. He pressed the starter. . . . Pray God it would start. The started whirred. . . . Nothing! He could hear someone run-ning. Desperately he pressed the starter again. Then the engine came to life. He revved up, slammed in the gear lever and, with tyres howling, shot out of the garage. Grogan was there, rounding the corner, knife in hand. Jake swung the Hillman through the gateway and spun the wheel to the right. Risking all, Grogan made a dive at the car and got a hand to the steering-wheel. Somehow he got his head through the window and hung on to the moving car tenaciously. Jake caught the stench of his breath as he screamed, "Stop, you sodding bastard, stop." It was no time for niceties. Jake lunged forward and with his left hand caught Grogan between the eyes. It was a full-blooded punch. The grip on the wheel loosened, and with a groan the man spreadeagled to the ground.

Jake put his foot down hard and switched on the head-lights. Merciful Jehu . . . surely the porter had said turn right. There, dead ahead and racing towards him at terrify-ing speed, was a high stone wall. He jammed on the brakes.

B

FIVE

MERCIFULLY, the brakes held. He knew it had been a damn-fool thing to go rocketing up the lane before switching on his headlights. The moonlight was all right as far as it went, but . . .

The car had pulled up a few feet short of the wall—at least he'd not crashed. Not that it made much difference now —with the wall in front of him, and Grogan down the lane! Grogan! Jake leapt from the car, whipped round to the boot and grabbed a spanner. Looking back, he could see Grogan still there, face down, some 30 or 40 yards away. Jake glanced around for a means of escape. It was only then he saw the trick his headlights had played on him; an illusion created by the sudden brilliance as the lights focused on the wall. Had he been going slower he would have seen it. No dead-end, no blind-alley, this. Certainly the wall was ahead of him, but what he hadn't at first noticed was that the lane—narrower than before—took a right-angled turn. So he was not trapped . . . he might yet get away with it.

He glanced back. Already Grogan was on his feet. Though the man was holding his head in his hands, Jake knew there was not a moment to lose. In an instant he was back in the car. He slammed it into gear and was off again without looking back. Was it imagination, or did he hear Grogan shout? Half a minute later he was round the Market Place and doing forty up the deserted *Vogelstraat*. He reached the motorway without difficulty, picked up the Brussels signpost, and, breathing a sigh of relief, settled himself in his seat. The luminous dial of his watch showed 2.30—it was unbelievable! Could so much have happened in a mere fifteen minutes?

Despite the hour, the motorway was not deserted, but traffic was light and well spaced out. He pushed his foot down and hoped the elderly Hillman would knock along indefinitely at sixty. Though he could see headlights in the mirror most of the time, there was no means of knowing if he was being followed. Surely, he thought, even the resourceful Grogan couldn't work miracles! It began to look as if Gostoli's packet would be delivered.

Dawn was breaking as he approached the outskirts of Brussels. Very soon he was entering the city, and cruising along an ample boulevard. His plan—his route—was worked out to the last detail, even to the laying of a false trail. He'd had ample time for this, back in the hotel bedroom. He'd located, and even memorised, the names of the streets which would take him to the Luxembourg road—*Boulevard Leopold II—Chaussee de Wavre*—then on to Namur, and, later, the diversion. . . . It was light enough now to read the street names—*Boulevard Leopold II* : right so far.

In the distance he saw the lights of a garage. He pulled in and filled up : thirty litres it took, and some oil. While the attendant was doing this, Jake eyed the road. Not a car in sight. He smiled, congratulating himself on his success, yet feeling some sense of disappointment that it had been so easy.

In Namur he saw a direction post—Dinant-Luxembourg —and then he was clear of the town. By now the character of the country was changing : he was entering the hilly, wooded area of the Ardennes, with its straggling villages of green-shuttered cottages. Some miles on, at the bottom of a gentle slope, a level-crossing came into view, its red and white poles across the road, barring the way. One car was already stopped, and soon others came to join the queue on either side of the railway line. At last the engine in the nearby station began to move forward. It passed by so close that he felt its heat and smelt its oiliness. So intent was he on the passing train that he was unaware that a small dark-green sports car had joined the waiting queue behind him. The driver was a girl—young, attractive and alone!

Now the red and white poles were raised, and as the rumble of the train faded the waiting cars roared away. Jake was now getting hungry, and he began to look for a place where he could pull off the road. A long straight road, bounded by woodland, stretched away before him : ideal for his purpose. Soon he saw a break in the trees, and a track leading into the woods. He slowed and turned into a tiny glade, where he was hidden from the road. Jumping out, he raced to the edge of the road and, hiding behind a large tree, watched the approaching traffic. For ten minutes he waited, and, though several cars went past, he was confident that none contained Grogan. He returned to the clearing, and was soon tackling the food and wine which the hotelier had thoughtfully provided.

Replete now, and content with his success, he yawned hugely. Stretching his legs across the passenger's seat, his eyelids began to droop, and almost at once he was asleep. Half a mile back, pulled off the road and blending with the colour of its surroundings, was a green sports car. The girl in the driving-seat lowered her field-glasses with a smile of satisfaction. Jake's movements had been closely followed.

It was afternoon before he awakened. He had been dreaming—the impossible had happened. Grogan had found him. He could feel his hand—so small and soft for such a lout—gently rousing him. Slowly, reluctantly even, he came up from the depths, and his imminent danger hit him before he was fully conscious. Instinctively he clutched the hand and held it in a grip of steel.

"Ouch ! Stop . . . you're hurting. . . ." It was a girl's voice.

Sleep vanished, and in a moment he was fully awake and gazing into the bluest eyes he'd ever seen. "God, I'm sorry," he muttered, releasing the hand. "I must have been dreaming."

"Not to worry." She was English all right. "Anyway, I'm

the one to apologise—waking you. Hardly pleasant, was it—the dream I mean?"

She was not beautiful in a classic way, but there was something about the sparkle of her eyes and her vivacity that matched so well her silken raven hair, and gave her a special radiance. To Jake, at this moment conscious of her nearness, she seemed utterly feminine and desirable.

He sat up in the driving-seat, for a moment at a loss. "I hope I didn't hurt you," he said.

"Forget it," she laughed, rubbing her hand ruefully. "My fault. Trouble is, I'm in a spot of bother . . . my car. It's broken down; probably out of petrol."

He leapt from the car, unable to believe his luck. " 'Fraid I don't carry a spare can, but I'll soon drive you to a garage and get some."

"That'd be marvellous." She smiled, and Jake was lost. "I was going to stop a passing motorist," she explained, "when I saw the gap in the trees and thought I could see a car. So here I am."

"Let's go and have a look, shall we?"

Following her out of the wood, he was lost in admiration. That gorgeous figure, those shapely legs! He felt his manhood surging within him. Once he held her arm as she stumbled in a deep rut. She looked up and laughed.

The car, an open green M.G., had stopped a yard or two up the road. They walked towards it.

"May I get in and try her?"

"Surely."

He lowered himself into the driving-seat, and the girl leaned across, pointing out the controls. Again he was conscious of her nearness: maddening and provocative. She reached over and switched on the ignition.

"You've got plenty of petrol," he said unsteadily. "The indicator shows nearly half a tank."

"Well—what is it, then?"

"Dunno—let's try her first." He grabbed the starter. The engine spun, but refused to fire.

"There you are," she said. "What did I tell you?"

He held the starter again, experimenting with the accelerator—nothing!

"Not a squeak," she said, shrugging her shoulders.

"Better look under the bonnet."

"Closed book to me."

He saw it in a moment—it was obvious. The clips holding down the distributor cap had come undone, and the thing was hanging down alongside the engine, suspended only by the leads.

"There's your trouble," he said proudly, clipping it back into position. "I'll bet she's O.K. now . . . can't think how that could happen though. . . ."

She lifted an eyebrow. "Yes, odd, isn't it? Maybe some damn fool mechanic. Had it serviced yesterday."

She got into the car, flicked the starter, and the engine leapt to life. "Great stuff. Aren't you clever?"

Too clever by half, thought Jake, frowning. In a minute she'd be off down the road, with perhaps a wave of the hand, and then *finis*.

She looked up, sensing his mood. "What's the matter?"

"Oh . . . nothing," he said abruptly. "Well, that's not strictly true. You see, we've only just met. It—it seems a pity you've, well . . ."

"Got to go?" she prompted, archly.

"Yes."

She gave a laugh. "O.K. then, let's defer the heartbreak. Get in the car, and we'll talk." She patted the seat at her side with a scarlet-tipped hand.

A strange silence came between them as they sat side by side. She was waiting, it seemed, for him to make the opening gambit.

"My name's Jake," he said at last. "Jake Standish."

Their eyes met, and she began to laugh. "I suppose that's as good a way as any," she rippled. "Anyway, mine's Petronella St Clair. Shocking mouthful, isn't it? Some call me Pet, but nearly everyone goes for Nella."

He gave a sideways glance. She couldn't be much over twenty, he thought.

She turned, watching a car race by at speed, throwing up a cloud of dust. . . .

"Oh . . . damn!" Her hand flew to her eye.

"What's the matter?"

"Hell! It's a bit of grit or something."

"Don't rub it," he urged. "Let's look."

He leaned across. "Yes," he cried, "I can see it. Let's have your handkerchief."

He held up the handkerchief triumphantly.

"Clever Jake," she murmured. "What should I do without you?"

Their heads were close together. She looked up at him with dancing eyes: her lips were only inches away. They were impossible to resist. His blood pounded, and he leant forward. . . .

Her head went back, and for a moment she lay passive in his arms. Her mouth was glorious, warm, soft, responsive. Then she pulled away.

"You're a fast worker," she said simply, straightening her scarf. "That wasn't in the contract, you know. I thought we got in the car to talk." Though her tone was serious, her eyes twinkled. He leaned forward again, emboldened. . . .

"You're to behave," she said quietly, holding him off, "or I shall go."

"I'm sorry," he said.

"That's all right, then," she replied in a matter-of-fact voice. After a pause she said, "You're an artist, aren't you?"

"How on earth?"

"Easy. I saw your easel in your car."

"Yes, I'm an artist," he replied. "I'm roaming . . . where the fancy takes me. Doing a few pictures."

Her eyes sparkled again. "What a coincidence. I'm roaming, too: no fixed itinerary. I'm supposed to be painting some water-colours . . . for a friend who's writing a . . . a sort of guide book." She held up her right hand, and he noticed a plastic finger-stall on her first finger. "Trouble is, I tried to break that off in the car door yesterday, so can't paint for a day or two."

"You *do* need looking after, don't you?"

"Tell you what," she said suddenly. "I've got some food with me. I'm hungry—let's share it, then we can talk. One doesn't meet a fellow artist every day, even if he is . . . a bit impulsive."

"You bet," purred Jake. "And I've got half a bottle of wine left. We'll make it a party.

SIX

OBLIVIOUS of the passing traffic, they sat in her car for over an hour. Sometimes they were serious, sometimes they laughed, but gradually he was induced to talk about himself. Though he told her much of his early days and his life in his West Kensington studio, his instinct warned him to keep silent as to his real reason for being abroad. She was a good listener, and it was difficult to get her started about herself. He could sense of certain reticence over this, which he put down to a reluctance to recall days which apparently had not been happy. It seemed her painting ability had developed from a natural aptitude, for, unlike Jake, she was completely untrained. She hesitated when he asked to see some of her work. "They . . . they are in my case," she told him. "Hardly worth showing . . . at least, not to an expert like you. Later, perhaps."

How it happened neither of them quite knew, but presently they decided they'd travel on together—at any rate as far as Liege. She expressed surprise when he told her he was making for Aachen : that he wanted to see Cologne, and then go on through the Rhineland. "But you're miles off route," she said, adding hurriedly, "That is . . . if you were going south."

"I came through Brussels, but I wanted to see the Ardennes," he replied casually.

When he got the Hillman out on to the road he had a sudden thought. He ran back to the M.G., already ticking over. "You *will* follow—won't you?" he asked anxiously. "No slipping off. Promise?"

She gave him a playful tap on the cheek. "Of course, silly."

A couple of kilometres down the road he found the turning —HOEI. LUIK. He swung the car round and looked in the mirror. A moment later the M.G. came into view. She was following, as promised. At Huy-sur-Meuse they stopped for a while to see the ancient citadel and, what was of special interest to Jake, the painted porcelain. It was early evening when they reached Liege.

Auberge de la Concorde—the name meant nothing to them. It was just one of the larger hotels in Liege, in the western part of the town. Jake chose it because it was easy of access and because it had an air of comfort and, it seemed, of gaiety. He felt gay. It wasn't often he met up with a girl like Nella, someone who attracted him enormously and who, miraculously, seemed well pleased with him.

The dining-room was crammed, and filled with the buzz of conversation. A touch of intimacy was lent by the soft glow of the shaded table-lamps. Jake gazed at the girl opposite him.

"Nella . . . you look wonderful."

This was an occasion, and she had determined to look her best. She had put on a short cocktail dress, the colour of old port, close-fitting and low-cut, showing off the provocative undulations of her breasts to perfection. She returned his gaze, for her part liking what she saw. There is strength of character there, she thought, yet kindness and compassion. A man like this oughtn't to be hurt. . . . She sighed. I'm a bitch. God—I'm a bitch, she mused.

Shaking off the mood, she gave him a wan smile. "Glad you like it," she said carelessly. "Anyway, you don't look so bad yourself."

Jake grinned. "The place, too . . . good choice, eh? . . . Happy and friendly. Matches our mood."

"Oh, yes," she lied. If only, she thought, I could give myself up to the enjoyment of the evening. Still—that was life. She'd got a job to do : there could be no drawing back. She drained the last of her liqueur and stubbed out her cigarette.

"I suppose we ought to be moving," she said at last.

Jake dragged his eyes away from her and glimpsed the empty tables. "I suppose so," he answered. "What'll we do?"

"How about a stroll? Get an eyeful of the town . . . have a drink somewhere, if you like."

It was already dark when they got outside, but the shop windows were brilliant with light and the boulevards crowded. Nella crooked an arm through his, and, as if by mutual consent, they turned away from the bright lights, and presently came to the river. Though the moon had not yet risen, the glow of the city bathed the scene in a pale opalescent light. At the bottom of a flight of stone steps they came to the very edge of the river. Below them the dark water lapped gently against the empty barges tied to their bollards. As they stopped and, hand in hand, gazed down into the purple depths, the girl turned towards him and looked up. The next moment she was in his arms and he was kissing her passionately. She gave her lips to him with an abandon which left him breathless—he could feel her lithe young body straining towards him, eager and responsive.

"Oh, Jake," she whispered. "Oh, Jake." He caught a tone of despair in her voice.

He drew back, concerned. Her face, mere inches from his, was pale and tense—the picture of wretchedness. "What is it, my darling?" he murmured.

Her expression changed, and she clung to him. "It's nothing, nothing at all. Kiss me again."

How long they clung to each other they neither knew nor cared. To Jake it was ecstasy; his world—one of thrills and caresses—stood still. Presently she laid her hands on his chest and pushed him gently away.

"We should go," she said unsteadily. Then, forcing herself, she went on lightly, "Let's get a drink somewhere. . . . I don't know about you, but I could do with one."

By the time they reached the boulevard again Nella had taken herself in hand; such things were not for her. She knew well enough already that it wouldn't take much for her to fall for this harum-scarum young artist. With an effort she shook off the thought—she had a job to do; whatever her personal feeling, she must get on with it.

In one of the main streets they found a place. There were a number of marble-topped tables set out, and in one corner, behind a plush-covered settle, they found one unoccupied.

"What'll we drink?" enquired Nella.

"What do you recommend?"

"Ever tried cognac and ginger ale?"

"No. Why . . . is it good?"

"Fabulous. You must try it . . . not too much ginger."

The drinks in front of them, they sat for a while in silence, neither, it seemed, anxious to talk. Nella sat very still, looking at that moment rather helpless. She took a sideways glance at Jake, who was gazing thoughtfully at nothing in particular. She guessed his thoughts, and knew she must make him snap out of it : she could not let him be hurt more than necessary. Presently she ventured : "Tell me more about your work, Jake."

"Damn the work," he exploded. He leant towards her and looked earnestly into her eyes. "Nella," he went on, "about this evening . . . about us. I must . . ."

"No, Jake." Her soft hand touched his. "Don't say a thing, darling. We're having fun; great fun . . . let's leave it at that."

"But that's ridiculous. You must know . . ."

Her voice hardened. "No, Jake . . . I beg you." Then, in a softer tone, "What happened just now was . . . great, but it's not for us. . . . Forget it."

"But, damn it . . ."

"Forget it . . . for tonight, anyway." Picking up her glass, she swallowed her drink at a gulp. "Cheer up," she advised, "and let's have another cognac . . . a fizzer!"

"I don't understand. . . ."

"Don't try," she said tartly. "Now, what about that drink?"

A fresh-faced *comme* brought the drinks, and went on his way. Conversation languished. Jake's thoughts were chaotic. Why should she want to fence him off? She'd been marvellous, so responsive, and now . . . Why the change? Why?

She was rummaging in her handbag. "Blast," she said suddenly. "I'm out of cigarettes. Get me a packet, there's a dear. Anything will do."

She watched his tall masculine figure as he threaded his way to the counter: how miserable he looked. She sighed, knowing what she had to do, and hating herself for it. Beneath the table she felt in her handbag and her fingers closed over a small glass phial. With a deft movement she snapped off the brittle top, and held the phial over his glass. . . .

"Here you are," said Jake, returning and throwing the cigarettes on to the table. "That's the best I could get."

"They'll be O.K.," she returned lightly, as she lifted her glass to her lips. "Cheers," she toasted him. "And no more miseries."

"Cheers," echoed Jake mechanically.

She watched him closely as he drank, but he made no comment. "Good stuff, this drink, don't you think?" she said. "A friend in Paris put me on to it."

His face clouded, and with an angry gesture he drank deeply. "Another man, I suppose," he said truculently.

"What's wrong with that?"

"Nothing, I suppose."

"As a matter of fact, it was a girl. But don't let's get scratchy."

For the next few minutes she worked hard, encouraging him to talk about his painting, anything and everything except about herself. Presently he yawned, and she guessed it was time to move.

"Come on," she said abruptly. "I'm getting tired. Time to go."

"O.K." He yawned again.

"You look tired, Jake. We've had a long day . . . let's get moving."

"I am tired," he confessed. "I feel all-in suddenly. Bloody stupid. . . ." He stifled another yawn.

She took his arm again as they strolled back to the hotel, and he was grateful for the support. Once he stumbled, and she urged him on.

"Can't think why I'm so tired," he muttered as they climbed the hotel steps.

Waiting for the lift, she had to support his sagging body —almost holding him up. "Must be the bloody drink," he murmured in a thick voice. "Feel damned ill."

Somehow she got him to his room and on to the bed. Then she worked swiftly. First she locked the door—she wanted no intruders. She removed his shoes easily enough, but she had to struggle to free him from his jacket. Then she loosened the collar of his shirt. . . .

For the most part he lay inert, breathing stertorously, but once, making a great effort, he tried to sit up, looking at her with unseeing eyes. It was as if he were trying desperately to fight off the drug—to tell her something. Twice he muttered something about Innsbruck; it sounded like "get Innsbruck". Another time, just before the drug finally took over, he mumbled incoherently. He seemed to be saying "grow down" or perhaps "grow can". She could make nothing of this, but his repeated reference to Innsbruck registered in her mind. Maybe that was where he was making for. "I shouldn't wonder at that," she said aloud. Presently, covering him with the bedclothes, she picked up the key of the room and let herself quietly on to the landing. She reached her own bedroom unobserved.

An hour later she returned. Jake was in a deep sleep, breathing regularly and in no way distressed. She was in the room no more than a few minutes, doing what had to be done. With a final sweeping glance to see that all was as it should be, she rearranged the bedclothes, put the key on the dressing-table, and left him for the night.

Back in her room, she lit a cigarette, picked up the telephone and asked for a Brussels number. Soon she heard the familiar voice at the other end. "It's Pet," she said simply.

"Yes."

"Everything's O.K."

"Good." He never said more than was necessary.

"I'm through," she went on hurriedly. "I've done what had to be done, and now I'm through."

"What the hell do you mean?"

"Just what I say . . . I've finished."

She heard him swear; could picture his face—puce with rage. "Cut that out," he exploded. "You've only done part of the job—you know that perfectly well. You're to stay and finish it. Do you hear?"

"I can't." There was desperation in her voice. "I won't . . . I won't do it."

"Gone soft, have you? Got sweet on the fellow, I suppose. Is that it?"

"Of course not. . . ."

"I should hope not. Business and pleasure don't mix—tell me your location."

"Liege. *Auberge de la Concorde*—in the *Boulevard Rosslyn*."

He didn't answer at once. Then—"I can't get to you tonight. Where'll you be tomorrow?"

"God knows."

"Listen. As soon as you know, ring me . . . see? I'll arrange to meet you some place. I'd rather collect it personally than use a D.L.B."

"Oh, all right." It was hopeless to argue.

"You're to stick to him—see the thing through to the finish. Savvy?" The line went dead.

She slammed down the receiver and, crossing the room, flung herself across the bed. "Oh, blast—blast—blast," she fumed, beating the pillow with her fists.

SEVEN

SOMEWHERE a bird was singing. The song floated in through the open window, filling the room with melody. To Jake's mind, still fogged by hours of unnatural sleep, it came through scrambled, discordant. Would it never stop? He longed to call out—tell it to shut up—but his muscles refused to mouth the words. The light from the window was intolerable. It hurt his eyes as he tried to open them. Why couldn't it remain dark for ever? He turned on his side, buried his head, and shut out the world.

When he awoke some two hours later the sun was pouring into the room. He felt drowsy, and hazy in his mind, but much refreshed. As he rubbed the sleep from his eyes his jumbled thoughts began to take shape. A fleeting vision came to him of a man lying spreadeagled in a lane, and he vaguely remembered the Hillman tearing through the night—head-lights ablaze. Then he heard the pant of a locomotive by a level-crossing, and glimpsed again the azure of the most beautiful eyes he'd ever seen—Nella! Remembering her, everything fell into place like the last pieces of a jig-saw.

He sat up in bed, his nerves suddenly tense. What could have happened? It took more than a couple of drinks to knock him out! The thought was ludicrous. Then, like a blow in the stomach, the truth hit him—he'd been drugged! But who—who—could have done this? There was only one answer. Trying desperately to believe himself wrong, he knew—Nella! Nella, play-acting, leading him on; with one object in mind—to secure the packet for Grogan. He shuddered, the thought revolting him. Fight against it as he would, everything pointed to his being right. The so-called chance meeting; the broken-down car; her despairing cry as they clung to each other by the river; it all added up. The packet?

His hand flew to his chest, grasping the chain about his neck. It was still there. Mystified, he lifted it over his head and held the packet in his hand. It was intact; the seal unbroken. He began to have doubts. Nella? How could it be? And yet . . . He roused himself, knowing what he must do : the uncertainty must be ended. He flung on his clothes and ran down to the floor below. Reaching her room, he hammered angrily. There was no reply. It was as he'd feared —she'd left! He hammered again. Silence. Now he was sure she'd gone : walked out on him. But the packet? Nothing seemed to make sense.

An aged chambermaid creeping past gave him an enquir-ing look. "Has Miss St Clair—in Room 200—left?" he asked anxiously.

The woman drew a master-key from her pocket. "We will see," she replied in a toneless voice. The door opened and she stood back to allow him to enter.

The room was in darkness, the thick curtains drawn across the window. In a flash he had flung them wide, and the sunlight flooded in.

Nella was in bed—sound asleep!

He turned to the crone hovering in the doorway. "Leave us," he commanded.

He looked down at the sleeping girl, his mind in a whirl. Surely, if she had drugged him, she would have taken the packet and cleared out. Yet the packet was intact—and she was here in bed, looking serene and utterly lovely. His anger died. Whoever she was, whatever she'd done, she was irresistible. As he watched, she stirred. Yawning, she threw an arm across her still-closed eyes. "The light," she mur-mured. "Turn out the light."

He crossed to the window and drew the curtain. His back was towards her, and he did not see the flicker of her eyelids as she took a momentary glance at him. Returning to the bed, he caught at her bare shoulder.

"Wake up, Nella," he said abruptly.

She opened her eyes and looked at him gravely. "Leave me," she said, her eyelids drooping. "I'm so tired."

He knew at once that something was wrong. He clutched at her arm. "No, Nella," he cried. "You must wake up."

Again she opened her eyes, slowly—painfully, it seemed—and gazed fixedly. It was as if he weren't there. He took her hand. "Listen. I must talk to you," he said. "Something's happened." She made no movement, no response. At last, without expression in her voice, she spoke. "Yes . . . I know." Then her eyelids drooped again. His brain suddenly came to life. There could be but one explanation. Nella too—*she'd* been drugged. But what was the sense of it? Why? Why?

He put an arm about her and raised her to a sitting position. He slapped her hard on the hand : slapped her cheek. "Come," he urged. "You must make the effort." Presently she roused. "Eh? What's the matter?" She held her head in her hands. "Oh, God," she groaned. "I feel awful."

"You've been drugged, that's why," he said. "We've both been drugged. Drugged—do you hear?"

"I'm so tired, Jake, please let me lie back."

She lay for some moments, her eyes open, her brow wrinkled. All at once she seemed to understand. "Drugged?" she murmured. "Why, that's silly—who'd do a thing like that?"

"I don't know yet, but I mean to find out."

"Masterful, aren't you?" she said, raising her hand to her cheek. He saw the smooth flesh pink where he'd slapped it, and was suddenly full of compassion. "Nella," he cried. "Oh, Nella . . . and I thought it was you. Thought you'd drugged me."

"Me?" She contrived a laugh : weak and silvery. "Whatever gave you that idea?"

"It was crazy, ridiculous, I know. . . ."

"But, Jake darling—why should I want to do that?"

Ten minutes ago he thought he had the answer. But now, looking into her face, so innocent, so lovely, he didn't know what to say. "You could have been doing it for somebody else, I suppose." It sounded lame, inadequate.

"But why?"

"There's a reason," he answered slowly. "But . . . well . . . let's forget all about it. It's not important."

"Something funny *is* going on. But if you don't want to talk about it, O.K." After a pause, she went on, "I thought it odd last night, when you passed out. Imagined you were, perhaps, subject to that sort of thing—blackouts and things, I mean."

"Not likely. I was drugged, I tell you."

"You were pretty far gone when I got you to bed," she continued, "but it wasn't until later, in my room, that I began to feel terrible. I couldn't understand it, but if what you say about drugging is correct, then it makes sense, perhaps. Don't you think it was the drink—gone off or something?"

"Brandy doesn't—what you call—go off. We were drugged."

"I don't believe it." They were bold words, but, looking at her, he could tell she was afraid. Suddenly she grasped his hand and snuggled closer. "Jake," she said in a quaking voice, "I hate this place. Let's get out of it."

"But last night . . ."

"I know, I know, but that was last night : before all this happened." She gave a shiver. "I'm frightened. Something's going on : I don't know what it is. We must go. Please, Jake . . . take me with you . . . we must go now. . . ."

Back in his room he brooded over the affair as he shaved. One thing was certain now : it wasn't Nella. But if it had been Grogan, why hadn't he taken the packet? He would have had an easy and bloodless victory. The more he thought about it all, the more mysterious it became. The packet . . . intact! It seemed so odd. His hand strayed to the chain around his neck. Even as he touched it he realised he'd been every kind of a fool : fancy carrying the thing around with him ! It was asking for trouble. But what was the alternative? The answer came in a flash. The car ! Hide it in the car— he knew the very place.

A handful of guests were already down when the lift deposited him on the ground floor. Round in the garage space at the rear of the hotel, and tucked away where he'd left it, was the Hillman. He climbed into the driving-seat, and, making sure he was not observed, he unclipped the packet from the chain around his neck. Fumbling with his hand under the passenger's seat, he found the small hole where the upholstery had split. It took only a moment to push the packet deep in among the springs and to rearrange the split leather. He smiled. No one would find it there.

He locked the car and was sauntering nonchalantly away when a thought occurred to him. The road-book in Nella's M.G. ! He knew that since last night's mystery it was more than ever necessary to travel by unfrequented roads. Some- how he must throw Grogan, or this unknown person, off the track. He remembered seeing this comprehensive road-book in Nella's car when they were having their alfresco meal in the Ardennes. This was just what was needed—and Nella wouldn't mind. He found the green M.G. in the covered part of the garage. Leaning over it, he felt in a side pocket for the book, but it was not there. As he was taking his hand away it came into contact with something cold, hard and unmistakable.

He looked furtively over his shoulder, probing every corner of the garage : no one was about. His fingers closed on the object and pulled it out. It was a revolver ! A small, silvery thing, this—ridiculously small—but with the name of a famous gunmaker on it. It lay in his hand, minute and shining : a toy of a thing. But this was no toy—he knew enough about guns to realise that. He flipped open the breach. The gun was fully loaded : each one of its chambers occupied by a lethal .22 bullet !

EIGHT

JAKE frowned. A suspicion of doubt again flickered in his mind. Was she really innocent?

He carefully replaced the gun, deciding it give the road-book a miss and to keep his mouth shut. It was a pensive and not entirely satisfied Jake who returned to the hotel. He had finished his breakfast when she came down, but at the sight of her his doubts vanished. Though she looked sparkling, it was plain from her general demeanour that she'd not fully recovered from her recent experience.

It was raining hard when they reached the little riverside town of Boppard in the early afternoon. The river, the sky, the distant view, all were blotted out. They'd had their fill of motoring for one day.

After leaving Liege they had made their way by unfrequented roads to Cologne, where they'd visited the Cathedral during their brief halt. There had been a short stop at the frontier, but to Jake's relief, after producing his passport and green card, there were no questions and he'd been casually waved on. After leaving Bonn they drove along roads high above the Rhine. Here the views of the river were quite wonderful, and he wished he could be sharing them with the girl. Surely it would have been more sensible to leave one car behind, or maybe to have parted company! But Nella had been determined: they must take both cars. As for parting company—she had implored, almost begged, that she be allowed to stay with him. Who was he to object? He found her enchanting: he'd have been an idiot to refuse.

During the drive his thoughts wandered back to Grogan and the packet. Life seemed so good just now, that he began to wonder how he could ever have felt bored. It did not occur to him that the wisest thing he could do would be to go back to England, tell Gostoli what he could do with his wretched stamp, and give him back his money. Instead, he was finding the whole thing stimulating : he'd undertaken to deliver the packet—and this he intended to do.

At Oberwinter they stopped for an alfresco lunch. Though the wine and food they'd bought in Bonn went down well, the girl seemed subdued and they talked little. It was warm in the sun at the water's edge, and they were content merely to watch the great barges haul their heavy loads up and down the river. There seemed to be no hurry : pursuit was improbable.

It was on the road near Koblenz that the rain began. At first a mere drizzle, it soon became a downpour, blotting out the landscape. After a few miles he stopped and went back to her car, where they sat arguing about what they should do. Nella said it was pointless to go on. "We'd be far better in a hotel. There are some wonderful views along this route— pity to miss them all." But Jake, vague thoughts of Grogan in his mind, was for pressing on. In the end they agreed to continue as far as Boppard where, if the weather had not improved, they would put up for the night.

The hotel by the river was small and looked comfortable enough, and they found a place at the back where they parked their cars. Jake, remembering where he'd hidden the packet, locked the Hillman's doors. Must be safe here, he thought, she's such an old warrior. Nella had the blues properly, and he was cross when she announced her intention of going to her room to write letters. "See you at dinner," she said, with a touch of petulance in her voice.

When some hours later she joined him for dinner, the mood had passed. She took his arm; reaching up on tiptoe, she put her mouth to his ear and whispered, "Sorry." Then they passed into the almost-empty dining-room. The food

and wine were good, and before the meal was half-over Jake
was delighted to see the clouds had rolled by and a watery
sun was appearing. "See," he said. "It's cleared. We may get
a stroll by the river presently."

She took his point, and looked up, laughing. "Maybe."
Her blue eyes dancing, she added, "You'd like that, wouldn't
you?"

"You bet."

"I admit I've been a bit stuffy today, Jake. I'll try and
make up for it presently."

It was while he was in the vestibule waiting for her to
come down that Jake noticed the man at the reception desk.
He was tall and erect. Jake could only see his profile, but
from the close-cropped greying hair and the round head, he
had a certain Germanic look. Moreover, from the guttural
sounds that came across, it seemed his conversation with the
reception clerk was in German. Watching them, Jake was
surprised to see the clerk point a finger in his direction. At
that moment Nella came down the stairs. "I forgot," she
called. "My mac's in the car. I'll run and fetch it. Then I'm
ready."

As they turned towards the door, the man approached
them.

"Pardon me," he said, in passable English. "But are you
the owner of car number XYZ 300?"

"Yes," replied Jake, surprised.

"I'm from the police," said the man, producing a card
with *Polizei* on it.

"Oh! Anything wrong?"

"We have found your car." The words came slowly, as if
he had difficulty in framing the sentence.

"What do you mean? My car's at the back of the hotel."

"*Nein,*" was the reply. "I beg your pardon. No, it is not
at the back of the hotel. We have found it . . . abandoned
. . . in a wood two or three kilometres distant."

Jake bit back an oath. So they'd got the car! Must have
known he'd hidden the packet. Had someone watched him?

"We knew it was a British car, naturally," went on the policeman. "I have already been to two other hotels, trying to find you. But do not worry . . . your car is not damaged."

Not damaged, thought Jake, but ransacked, of course! It seemed he could never do the right thing.

During the conversation Nella had remained quiet. Now she spoke. "Why on earth should they take your car?" she asked.

The policeman was talking again. "I have left a man with it, Herr . . .?

"Standish."

"It is quite safe, Herr Standish. Will you please to come with me and collect it."

"Very well." Perhaps there was just a chance they'd not found the packet. Highly improbable : the Grogans of this world were taught to be thorough—he must have found out : had him watched. Oh, hell!

"I'll come with you," said Nella.

Their companion shrugged his shoulders. "As you wish," he said. "But there is no need."

"Nevertheless, I'll come," replied Nella bluntly. "I'll just get my macintosh from my car."

The man frowned, chafing at the delay. "That will not be necessary," he said. "I have a . . . limousine outside." But Nella had already gone.

A black Mercedes was drawn up outside the door of the hotel. Within moments Nella reappeared, struggling into a smart red raincoat. "I'm ready now," she said.

"We go then," replied the German irritably, flicking the engine into life.

Fifty yards back another car—a dark-blue Citroen—was parked. In it were two men : an evil-looking pair. The driver, insignificant and puny, had an Oriental appearance with shifty, slanting eyes set in a pock-marked face. Abject fear was etched in every facet of his countenance, and the hands which held the wheel were trembling. The appearance of his companion, bald, giant-like almost, could only be described as grotesque. Enormous gristly ears projected from his polished cranium, and on either side of his face ran deep scar-like lines reaching from his nostrils to the edge of his mouth. He had a loose bottom lip, curled and fleshy, whilst the top—a hare-lip—twisted at the corner, gave him a sinister, almost terrifying appearance.

The sight of the Mercedes pulling away from the hotel galvanised the bully into instant action. "After 'em, Poxy," he screamed, "and, by Christ, I'll have the knackers off you if you lose him this time." But already the Citroen was in pursuit.

Meanwhile the Merc was quickly out on the open road and surging forward. A thoughtful Jake was wondering how Grogan could possibly have caught up with him. How could he have found the car? When did he take it from the hotel car park? He took a glance at Nella, sitting thoughtfully by his side. Again that feeling of unease about her came over him. Surely not! It didn't seem possible. He turned to the driver. "How did you come to find the car?" he asked.

"These things happen."

Another kilometre down the road, they slowed and turned off at right angles into what was little more than a lane. "Soon be there," said the man.

The rounded a corner, and just ahead Jake noticed a thicket at the side of the road. There was a rough track leading into it : it reminded him of the wood where he'd met Nella. The car pulled up with a jerk. "This is it," said the policeman abruptly, indicating that they should get out. Jake took the girl's arm and followed the man into the thicket. There was an eerie silence about the place, broken only by the drip, drip from the rain-soaked trees overhead. The policemen fell back behind them and, as they rounded the bend, there in a clearing stood the Hillman. Then, too late, he saw something else. He whipped round. . . .

"Keep walking," said the *soi-disant* policeman, his knuckles showing white as he gripped a big .38 Colt in his hand. Jake kept walking: so too, her face expressionless, did Nella.

The door of the Hillman was open. Inside, a heavily built man, chewing the butt end of a cigar, lay across the front seats. But long before he climbed out and lumbered towards them, Jake knew. . . .

"So!" said Grogan, raising an arm and flipping him a savage back-hander across the mouth. "So—we meet again."

NINE

IT WAS an unlucky blow. It sent Jake reeling back; his foot caught against a sawn-off tree trunk, and he fell heavily. Nella gave a cry and ran towards him. "Keep out of this, you," screeched Grogan, sweeping her roughly aside.

Jake got to his feet, and shot her a look of gratitude. "I'm all right, Nella," he said, feeling far from it. There was an excruciating pain in his back, and already blood was pouring from his lips. He reached for a handkerchief to staunch the flow.

"Not bleeding likely, you don't," yelled Grogan. "You keep those mitts away from your pocket."

It had all happened so quickly that it was only then that Jake was able to take a good look at him, and notice the half-closed eye and the great purple bruise down one side of his face. The sight of Grogan's features heartened him— so this was what he'd got for trying to stop the Hillman in Bruges. Jake smiled. The fellow must have read his thoughts. "Aye," he flashed, "you can laugh, but we haven't started on you yet." He turned to his companion and gave a painful grin. "Good work, Chesney," he shouted. "What an actor!"

So this was Chesney. But Jake already knew it must be so. To think that he should have fallen for it: how they must be laughing! Yet how could he have known? He'd only seen the man's back view; and as for the voice—well, nothing easier.

"A bit of education's always handy," remarked Chesney, keeping the .38 at the ready.

Jake shivered. It was cold and wet under the trees, and already the light was going. His lips were bleeding profusely, and every time he moved an agonising pain shot down his spine. In this condition what chance had he—even with his training—of making a break: what chance against Chesney's .38 and Grogan's gorilla-like arms?

Grogan was talking again. "No time to waste," he piped, his voice incongruous against his powerful body. Advancing on Jake, he lashed out again to his face with a heavy hand. "Come on, you," he cried. "Hand over. . . . I want the goods. . . . Pronto."

So they'd not found it! They couldn't have searched the car: it was safe so far. The thought brought a measure of comfort. He smiled. God, how his mouth hurt! . . . He stole a glance at Nella, tight-lipped beside him. What was going on inside that head. Their eyes met and she smiled. The smile, reassuring and friendly, lent him strength.

"I don't understand. . . ."

Grogan raised his fist. "Come on," he screeched, "we've no time to waste."

"Tell him to go to hell, Jake." It was the first time she'd spoken. But it was a Nella he'd never heard before : a voice resolute, commanding.

Grogan turned, his mouth twitching. "So the tart wants to play, too," he yelled. "We got ways of dealing with this." He beckoned to Chesney. "Keep 'em covered," he ordered, "while I rip off Red Riding Hood's coat . . . then the skirt . . ."

Chesney gave a guffaw.

Jake winced. So that was it : they'd get at him through Nella. Strip off her clothes. He knew this was no idle threat. Fury raged within him at the thought. He'd come into this thing for kicks, yet now he'd got an unlucky fall and balled up everything. What could he do against them? If he made a move Chesney would shoot: maybe at Nella even. He looked across at her. How unconcerned she looked, yet he daren't risk her getting hurt. Had he strength enough to pull off a surprise? He could only string them along, hoping his chance would come.

"What do you want to know?" he said.

"No," shouted Nella. "See them in hell first. Tell them to find it . . . if they can."

Grogan rounded on her, beside himself. "We'll see about that," he screeched.

Jake knew it was now or never. He lurched forward. "Keep your hands off . . ." The sudden movement brought an agonising pain to his spine. The sweat sprang to his temples. . . . But it was the crash of the explosion, terrifying in its nearness, that stopped him. He heard the whistle of the bullet and the dull thud as it buried itself in a near-by tree trunk. He heard, too, Chesney's howl of pain, and, turning, saw him spin round; saw the .38 drop from his mangled hand. Stunned at the turn of events, he saw the agonised expression on Chesney's face and, as in a dream, watched the blood spurt.

Two men had come running in from the road—one huge, ugly and cadaverous; the other insignificant, yellow, pock-marked. "After him, Poxy," yelled the big man, as Grogan, bandy legs flying, raced for cover.

"O.K., Boss," cried Poxy, dashing into the undergrowth in pursuit.

Taking no more than a contemptuous glance in Chesney's direction, 'The Boss'—revolver in hand—advanced on Jake. "Now then . . ." he began. At that moment the sound of two shots came from the far side of the coppice. 'The Boss' stopped in his tracks, listening hard. An instant later, a third shot, more distant than the others, echoed among the trees. The momentary silence which followed was broken by Chesney. "For God's sake, do something, Mister," he wailed, "before I bleed to death." It was obvious he was in a bad way. Even in the failing light Jake could see that the handkerchief round his hand was a crimson ball.

"You'll live," said the newcomer without turning. Then, fixing Jake with an icy stare, he said roughly, "Hand it over, and quick about it."

It was incomprehensible! First Grogan, now this hideous giant. How many more of them? The tempo of it, too! He had been congratulating himself on this unexpected deliverance; been about to thank this unknown rescuer even. Now, it seemed, he had another enemy: another, a damn sight more dangerous than Grogan, by the look of him. He could expect no quarter here. But who was he? How did he fit in with Gostoli's treasure? And Nella, too—he'd almost forgotten her; events had moved so fast. She must know something! Know about the packet. What was it she'd cried? Something about "Tell them to find it . . . if they can."

Even as these thoughts flashed through his mind she came to his side. It seemed she had not heard what the man said, for she came forward smiling and with her hand held out. He saw her face cloud when, as she said "Thanks for your help", 'The Boss' raised his gun and pointed it at her.

Then it happened. It was so quick, so unexpected, that the man was caught unprepared. The split-second lapse cost him the trick, for, quick as light, Nella cracked him hard under the wrist with her forearm. The blow, more powerful than it looked, jerked his hand up, and the gun flew into the air and fell to the ground. At the same time, perfectly co-ordinated—the other hand whipped from her mackintosh pocket. In it Jake saw the little silvered .22 glistening in the last of the daylight.

Standing back a pace, her face tense, Nella snapped, "One move, Boss, and your own mother won't recognise you."

Desperate men take desperate measures. She wouldn't shoot, he thought, lunging forward to seize her gun. But Nella, anticipating his reaction, stepped neatly aside and pressed the trigger. The bullet whistled past, missing him by inches. "Next time you'll die." The voice was icy.

"Christ." The man got the message.

Then Jake heard her voice again, urgent, authoritative. "Quick, Jake . . . their guns, both of them. Get your car, back it out on to the road and wait for me."

It was no easy matter—his back was hell: the least movement was agony. Yet somehow he retrieved the guns; first the Boss's, then Chesney's. As he moved towards the car she called, again in a crisp voice, "Give me one . . . keep the other. If they try any tricks, shoot."

Faint with the effort, he struggled to the car and slumped into the driving-seat. Black spots danced before his eyes, but somehow he manoeuvred it back along the track. "Attaboy!" she called, as he passed. It was like a clip from a film—Chesney, face contorted, holding his bleeding hand; 'The Boss', arms high above his head, fuming; and Nella, a gun in each hand, grim, unconcerned.

At last the Hillman was out in the road. The darkness was gathering. Below him, not a mile away, the lights of cars on the highroad flickered in and out—civilisation again: and all thanks to Nella. He switched on the head-lights and noticed a dark-blue Citroen pulled up against the grass verge. Boss's car, he thought. He looked back to the coppice. . . .

A moment later he saw her, a dim shadow walking back-wards, treading carefully. "Any funny business, and you're dead men."

Then she was beside him. "Quick, Jake," she urged. "To the hotel, and drive like blazes." He let in the clutch. The back axle howled and the car lurched forward. A moment later the coppice had passed from view, and then they were on the main road. He drove by instinct, striving to conquer the vertigo engulfing him. Though a hundred questions came to mind, he was beyond caring.

Her voice, mildly reproachful, broke the silence. "The petrol gauge, Jake," she cried. "The tank's empty."

He glanced at the dashboard. "Oh, God," he groaned. "I forgot to fill her up this afternoon."

"Keep going," she answered cheerfully. "We'll make it."

Soon the lights of the town came into view. He drove the car round to the back of the hotel and switched off the engine. "Made it," he gasped, his body going slack.

Reaching the foot of the stairs, Nella let go his arm. "Sure you can manage by yourself?" she asked. "If so, I'll try and get a lock-up for the Hillman. Then I'll come up and do some repair work on you."

When he reached his room he lowered himself on to the bed and closed his eyes. She came in quietly, but he didn't wake until she spoke. " 'Fraid I couldn't get a lock-up," she said, "but I've locked the car. The key's here, on the dressing-table." She had a first-aid box with her, and soon she was gently sponging his swollen lips. He winced when it came to the disinfectant. "Sorry, darling," she whispered, "but it's a must . . . it's all badly torn, and we can't be too careful." With dexterous fingers she dressed the wound. When it was done, his lips felt like balloons—but the better for her ministerings.

She soon had him undressed, laughing at his protests—then cool fingers were gently massaging his vertebrae. It was comforting. "Nothing broken," she murmured professionally, "but badly bruised." Finally she crossed to the dressing-table and picked up a brimming wine-glass. "Drink this . . . you'll feel better." He felt too unwell to argue, but the whisky brought new life to him. He could feel the warmth of it reaching out, comforting him.

She took the empty glass from him—then, hesitating a moment, she leaned over and brushed his cheek with her lips. "Sleep now," she whispered. "You'll feel fine by morning."

As she turned away he clutched at her arm. "Don't go yet, Nella," he begged. "Please don't go. Tell me . . . who are you? How do you know about—you know what? Why do you carry a gun?" The questions spilled out like a torrent.

Making no attempt to move, she stood at the side of the bed, silent, her head averted. What was he to her? How different she looked now from the young woman in the clearing—mouth set, a brace of guns at the ready. About her face now was a softness, a sadness, he'd seen but once in those unforgettable moments on that first night.

Presently she inclined her head, and their eyes met. "Please, Jake . . . no questions. Not tonight . . . perhaps tomorrow." She moved to go, but he gave a cry and struggled to sit up. The sudden movement sent a jagged pain up his spine, and he fell back with a muttered curse. Then she was on her knees, her arms around him, holding him tight. "Oh, Jake. . . . Oh, my darling," she murmured again and again. For a while she lay with her lips to his cheek, then, releasing him suddenly, she ran to the door. She looked back and, with her face contorted, cried out wildly, "I'm no good to you, Jake. . . ." Her hand flew to her mouth to hold back the words: he could see the struggle she was having to control her emotion. Then, her voice calming, she said quietly, "I'll shut the door after me. It's self-locking. On no account open it to anyone . . . to anyone . . . do you hear?" Before he could reply, she was gone.

Though dead-beat, sleep evaded him. There was so much he did not understand; so much to find out. Questions kaleidoscoped before him. Who was this girl who'd come into his life? Who was she working for? By her own admission, she'd said she was no good to him. How long he lay there, restless in mind and body, he neither knew nor cared. Somewhere a clock struck the hour, but long before the chimes ceased he had lost interest. Presently his thoughts strayed to Grogan, and then to the packet. Good grief! The packet—where was it? Events had moved so fast that the packet had been forgotten. He sat up in the bed, wincing with pain. What was it Grogan had said? "Hand over. . . ." Then he'd obviously not found it. Therefore it was still there—tucked away under the passenger seat. He sank back, exhausted: it was all so complicated, his mind boggled. In his weakness, anxiety about the packet assumed

c

huge proportions : became the most important thing in his life. He must know what had happened . . . where it was. Must find out now . . . tonight . . . this instant.

A cool wind was blowing in from the river as, sweating from exertion, he came out into the night. He shivered. The moon, riding high, gave the scene a pale unearthly radiance. Walking with difficulty, he made his way to the rear of the hotel, and in the pallid light caught the familiar shape of the Hillman. His hand trembled as he found the keyhole. The door swung open, and he was inside. In an instant his hand was under the passenger seat, fumbling. . . . Could it be that, after all, Grogan had found it; been playing some obscure game of bluff? He plunged his hand deeper among the springs, and then, giving a muffled cry of triumph, he felt its familiar shape. No need to look at it, he'd handled it so many times. Dangerous to waste time, he thought; must get back to his room—there were enemies everywhere. As he crossed the parking-place—the packet pocketed—the moon went behind a cloud. Like a blind man feeling his way, he reached the road, but as he turned towards the hotel he stopped dead. In the distance a dog barked. His muscles froze as he stood listening. He could hear voices— subdued voices—then footsteps. . . .

It was getting brighter. As he wedged himself in behind a brick pillar, the moon reappeared. Leaning forward, he saw two figures at the foot of the hotel steps. He watched them cross to a car on the opposite side of the street. Their voices, muffled by distance, reached him, but he could make nothing of their conversation. Only one thing was certain; it was a man and a woman. Lovers, no doubt.

Suddenly, carried towards him by the breeze, he heard the man's voice, unmistakably clear. "No matter what happens—you stick to him. Like a limpet . . . understand?" Then a starter whirred and the car glided away into the night.

Jake leaned forward. Then he knew. . . . That figure,

that walk! He would have known it anywhere. She came back across the road with dragging footsteps, slowly climbed the hotel steps and passed from view.

TEN

JAKE leaned back against the pillar, badly shaken. Must give Nella a few minutes to reach her room, he thought; never do to run into her. Too many questions would inevitably follow—questions they'd both want to ask. Better she believed him asleep in his room, and better, too, that she should not know he'd witnessed this meeting. Who was the man, and what was he to her? He felt a twinge of jealousy, even though he knew. deep down, that she was up to no good. The words—her own words, blurted out emotionally, came back to him. Then there were the words of the man—"Stick to him. . . like a limpet."

What was going on? And how did Nella fit into it all? He'd asked himself the question a dozen times. One thing was clear—she could not be connected with Grogan, otherwise she'd never have acted as she did. They could hardly have been playing some elaborate game of bluff especially for his benefit. No, Grogan's fury had been genuine. Equally, he didn't believe there was any liaison between her and the man he knew as 'The Boss'. Here, too, the fellow's surprise and chagrin at being outwitted had been no play-acting. There could only be one explanation. She and this midnight visitor must be hatching some plot against him, and if he, Jake, had any sense, the best thing he could do would be to clear out.

God, how weary he felt; his aching body had taken more than enough. Glancing down the deserted street, he stepped out into the moonlight and moved cautiously towards the hotel.

He awakened slowly. A thin beam of light from a gap in the curtains told him it was morning. He switched on a light and looked at his watch—six o'clock! He'd slept solidly since midnight, and was feeling better for it. He stretched, moving slowly, testing his back. It felt numb and bruised, but, miraculously, the acute pain of the previous night had eased. His mouth, though better, was still uncomfortable, but in spite of the sticking-plaster he could move his lips. The sleep, deep and untroubled, had done its work well.

Now the events of the past few days came flooding in. Gostoli, Grogan, Chesney, 'The Boss', Nella, each came in for a searching examination. He wondered what had happened to Grogan and 'Poxy'. He remembered the shots he'd heard at the other side of the copse, and wondered who'd bought it! Chesney, too; had he bled to death? And Nella? What was he to do about her?

A clock in the town was striking seven as he came to a decision. It was hard—almost unbearable to think about—but he knew he must steel himself. Even as he did so, he wondered if he was really in love with her : if he could go through with it. He sighed deeply, knowing there was no alternative. He must go now . . . leave her . . . get off before she left her room. He'd get away from the hotel and drive straight through to Innsbruck : not much over three hundred miles. Time he got moving, anyway; he would be a fool to hang about : get the thing over and done with. Maybe later he'd try to find Nella again.

The decision made, he dressed quickly. His back began aching again, but he'd just have to put up with it. The reception girl showed surprise when he reached her desk and asked for his bill.

"I've been called away on urgent business," he told her, adding, "Can't stop for breakfast. Perhaps you will explain to Miss St Clair . . . about the urgent business, I mean. She'll understand."

In the car park he found the Hillman. It had not been tampered with. Remembering the almost-empty tank, he drove straight round to the petrol pumps next to the hotel. "Put in all she'll take," he told the attendant, an intelligent youth speaking passable English. "I've a long journey ahead, and I don't want to stop too often." While the petrol was going in he glanced up at the windows of the hotel. He judged Nella's to be the farthest away, and he smiled grimly, noting the closed curtains. But he looked away too quickly, for a moment later a curtain was flung aside and a figure appeared at the window.

"Ulm?" he asked, as he paid the boy. "I turn left at the top of the hill, I think."

The lad gave a grin. "Yep," he answered.

Eight o'clock was striking as Jake pulled away from the pumps. "Not bad," he murmured to himself. A few minutes later he was on the road to Darmstadt, where he would join the autobahn. His plan was to go to Ulm, then branch off to Fussen and Innsbruck. Pity, he thought, I shan't have a chance to stop off at Ulm: always wanted to see the place —still, far better go right through to Innsbruck.

Soon after Mainz he found a road-house. It was 9.15, and he was hungry. He ran the car round out of sight of the highway—an obvious but simple precaution! A typical German fraulein served him with steaming coffee and crusty rolls. He was the only customer, and she lingered, chatting, while he ate. The time passed pleasantly, and he stopped longer than he intended. At Darmstadt he picked up the autobahn, and the Hillman began to eat up the miles.

Presently driving became boring, and he began thinking again about Nella. He told himself he'd panicked and had behaved like a damned fool to go running off without even writing a note of explanation. God, how he was going to miss her! It was all very well to say he'd meet her again after he'd finished the job. But the world was a large place —perhaps he'd never find her.

The kilometres flew by. The Hillman was running perfectly, and it was with a sense of achievement that at about 1 o'clock he realised he was only 15 kilometres from Ulm. Over 200 miles done since he left Boppard. He smiled, believing himself free from possible pursuers. It hadn't proved too difficult, after all. Grogan and Co. outwitted! He could imagine their fury. But then his face took on a puzzled look. Hardly get troubled by Grogan, in any case . . . probably shot. But perhaps get followed by 'The Boss' —doubtful, very! He passed another road sign—Ulm 5 km. It was all too easy.

Then he heard the Hillman cough.

It took the car half an hour to limp into Ulm, where he found a garage. The proprietor, explaining that he'd been a P.O.W. at Devizes, shook hands warmly and said he'd do anything he could to help. Jake fumed while a preliminary examination was made, and his spirits sank when told that the trouble was a burnt-out valve.

"How long will that take?"

"Ach! I regret I have no man available until later this afternoon."

"But it is important I get away as soon as . . ."

"For you, *Mein Herr*," broke in the man, "I will get it done by late this evening—though it will mean a very special effort."

It was a serious delay—he'd hoped to get through to Innsbruck before nightfall. Now he'd have to travel through the night. "If that is the best you can do," he said wearily. Then, feeling he'd been ungracious, he smiled and said, "I'm very grateful. And now, perhaps you can recommend a hotel where I can pass the time . . . have a bath and an evening meal."

"There are many in Ulm."

"One will do."

"Then I know just the place—the Hotel Laurent. It should do you very well."

Glad to stretch his legs in the sunshine and take some of the stiffness from his aching back, Jake enjoyed the short walk. He had no difficulty in finding the hotel. It was not large, but its colour-washed exterior and gay window-boxes appealed to him. The garage man had promised the car would be sent round to the hotel when it was ready, so now all he had to do was to get agreement to his passing a few hours there. He should be on the road again after dinner.

An elegant young woman came from an inner office, and with an attractive smile said something he could not understand.

"*Ich bin ein Engländer,*" he explained. It was a stand-by phrase.

She laughed. "Oh! You are English—my husband will be delighted."

Jake explained that his car had broken down, and told her his needs. "If I could have a room for a few hours . . . a bath, perhaps—and dinner?"

She wrinkled her brow. "A bath, dinner—yes. But a room? You see . . . we are expecting a coach soon. A room will be difficult. But wait . . . I will ask my husband."

He watched her go back to the inner room, and heard a murmur of conversation. He caught a glimpse of a man sitting at a desk. There was something about him that seemed vaguely familiar. Then the man got up from the desk, turned, and, with an easy stride, came towards him. . . .

"Jake!" he cried, his face beaming, his arms outstretched. "Jake, you old devil . . . what in hell's name brings you here?"

"Nicco!" gasped Jake. "Nicco Bullivant."

ELEVEN

It was ten years since they'd met : ten years since Attenborra's. For a time they'd exchanged letters, but after a
while this had ceased. At the sight of his old school-friend,
still bubbling over with that same bonhomie, Jake's spirits
rose. Here, at last, was someone with whom he could share
his problem : a faithful ally.

Lifting the flap of the desk which separated them, Nicco
bore down on him with all his old exuberance, and flung
his arms around him. Then he turned to the smiling young
woman. "Cilli," he cried, "this is Jake Standish—we've
often talked about him. Regular tearaway in his time." He
stood back and, noticing the sticking-plaster and the swollen
lips, cocked an eyebrow. "Not still fighting?" he asked.
"What the hell have you done to yourself?"

Jake laughed. "I didn't do it. Somebody else did. But it's
a long story . . . it can wait."

Then the floodgates opened.

Nicco started. "What have you been doing with yourself,
old boy, since we left Attenborra's? An artist, eh? Always
were good at drawing. Remember the sketches on the black-
board? Damned good—not always appreciated."

"What about you? You and your impersonations of the
Head. So this is your wife? Always were lucky with girls.
Knew you were somewhere in Germany, and had settled
down—but didn't know you owned a hotel. Lucky chap."

"Wife's place, not mine," answered Nicco, grinning.

"Married the owner's daughter. Poor old fellow died. Hung up me hat, eh, darling?"

At last, when the first exuberance had spent itself, Nicco became practical. "Of course you must stay here," he said. "Stay as long as you like . . . on the house, naturally. Longer the better, eh, Cilli?"

His wife gave a smile, infectious and warming. "Of course," she said quietly. Here, thought Jake, was the perfect foil for the explosive Nicco—a woman, calm, responsible and elegant.

Jake shook his head. "Very decent of you . . . but it can't be done. I'd like to stay for dinner, though." Glancing over his shoulder, he went on, "Can't tell you anything here, but if we can have a yarn presently? You see, I've to get . . . somewhere. And I must get there without delay."

"All very mysterious," said Nicco.

"It's a serious matter, believe me. But if we could have a talk . . . in private, I mean."

Taking Jake by the arm, Nicco led him towards a door across the entrance hall. Turning, he called, "Let me know, Cilli, when the coach arrives." And to Jake, "Too much for one to cope with. They come in a bloody horde."

They passed into a tastefully furnished room. Through the open window came the heavy scent of flowers from the window-boxes. Nicco pointed to one of the deep armchairs. "Not rheumatism, surely?" he asked, as Jake lowered himself gingerly.

"Nope. But wait until you hear the story; then you'll understand."

"I can't wait."

"Sure we can't be overheard?" asked Jake, glancing towards the window. "Enemies seem to turn up in the most unexpected places."

"Don't be daft," returned the other. Nevertheless, he got up and closed the window. As he came back, his blue eyes dancing, the sunlight caught his fair curly hair. As good-

looking as ever, mused Jake. Nicco and the charming Cilli
—they made a handsome couple!

Then Jake started. He described how boring life had
become in the West Kensington studio, and how, to seek
excitement, he'd stuck the advertisement in the Personal
column : more for a lark than anything else, he supposed.

"Of all the damn fool things. . . ."

Ignoring the interruption, the story went on. Gostoli—
the packet—the reward—nothing was forgotten. Living the
moments again, Jake told of the meeting with Grogan on
the boat—the voices behind the tree at Bruges—the midnight vigil in the shrubbery, and the escape to Brussels.
Nicco smiled when he got to the bit about Nella's broken-
down car. Jake pressed on to the drugging—to Nella's
anxiety lest he should leave her—to her gun—to the trap
in the thicket—to the arrival of 'The Boss' and Poxy, and
finally, after Nella's rescue work, to his decision to go-it-
alone.

For a moment Nicco said nothing. Then his face creased.
"You certainly gotten yourself into something," he laughed.
"Of all the prize idiots. . . ."

At this instant the door opened. "The coach has arrived,"
announced Cilli quietly.

"O.K., darling," said Nicco. He got up and moved to the
door. Turning to Jake, he said slowly, "This requires
thought. Look . . . I'll fix you up with a room, so you can
have that bath you're clamouring for. Later, when we've
got the crowd under control, we'll have another session.
Sure we'll be able to sort something out."

The hot bath was wonderful. As he lay back in the
steaming water a feeling of relaxation came over him; he
could feel the warmth of it drawing the pain from his back.
He felt at ease in mind and body : glad he'd unburdened
himself to Nicco. Together it would be an easy matter.

It wasn't until after dinner that they were able to resume
their talk. The man from the garage had brought the car
over, and when Jake got back into the hotel after settling

the account, Nicco appeared and took him by the arm. "Let's get back to the sitting-room," he said. "I've got some ideas." There was enthusiasm in his voice.

As they went into the room Jake shot a glance at the now curtained window. "Not to worry," said Nicco, turning the key of the door. "The window's shut—no one'll hear us."

They flopped into chairs. "Well?" said Jake expectantly.

"I've thought about this a lot," began Nicco. "Fascinating, I call it . . . fascinating." Jake waited, and Nicco continued. "I'm going to make one thing clear to you right away . . . that packet . . . *we're going to get it through*."

"We?"

"Certainly. It's to be a joint effort from now on."

"Good show."

"Listen. We know Grogan and what's-his-name—Chesney, are working for an unknown character named Larry. And we know that if they get the stamp, or whatever's in the packet, it is to be sold to the highest bidder."

"You don't think it's a stamp, then? Gostoli was a stamp dealer, you know."

"So you said. It may be a stamp, but it could just as easily be something else. Our first job is to find out—we must open it."

"No!" Jake insisted. "It must be delivered intact, otherwise the buyer won't accept it." Seeing the smile on his companion's face, he added hurriedly, "And don't suggest faking another seal. I won't have it messed about."

Nicco didn't argue. "It's not important," he said. "What is important is the number of people who are interested in it. You told me Poxy had the look of a Chinese about him —did it ever occur to you that you might be carrying something of international importance—important, say, to China?"

"Surely not. If it was that vital, why bring me—an outsider, an amateur—into it? Too risky. It's a professional job."

"On the contrary . . . just the sort of guy nobody would suspect."

"Go on."

"All right, then. We've established that two separate gangs are after the loot. That's certain."

"I knew that much already."

"Patience. We must get the certainties out of the way."

"What about the girl?"

"I'm coming to her. She's more difficult. It's my guess, Jake," he paused, "that the girl's crazy about you."

Jake's pipe almost slipped from his fingers. "Holy Moses! Do you really think . . ."

"Sure thing. All this stuff about not being alone. . . . She's bound to be in the swindle somewhere—doing a job. And part of that job is to hang on to you. But my belief is that she can't bear the thought of losing you—for herself, I mean—and is terrified you might get hurt."

Jake sat back, recalling the more intimate moments with her. "I wonder . . ." he murmured dreamily.

"And what is more," went on Nicco, "I know bloody well that you're crackers about her yourself—only you're too dumb to realise it."

"Perhaps I am," said Jake laconically. "Doesn't help much though, does it?"

"We'll forget the girl for now. Let's put her down as an unknown quantity. Anyway, you've got rid of her pretty successfully—which is what you wanted, presumably—so let's get back to the packet."

Jake sighed, and Nicco went on, "You're sure nobody followed you here?"

"Well . . . I didn't see anyone."

"Doesn't prove a thing; still, here's hoping. Now listen. My plan is that I should take the packet to Innsbruck for you. No one will connect me—a casual innkeeper—with the business."

"What do I do?"

"You go to Innsbruck first, without the packet. I follow later."

"And if I'm caught, they beat me up until I tell them you've got it. So that doesn't help. In any case, I'm not intending to take many more beatings-up. I know I came into this for excitement, but things are getting a bit too hot, and I bar getting bumped off and dumped in the river if I refuse to co-operate."

"You've got to do something to earn your money, you know."

"True . . . but there are limits."

Nicco inhaled deeply. "Perhaps it wasn't a good idea, after all," he said at length.

Suddenly Jake leant forward. "I know . . . What about a dummy packet? Would that help?"

"That's an idea. Just a moment while I think."

It was more than a minute before Nicco spoke again. Then, "Got it," he cried, clicking a finger and thumb. "We'll make up a dummy packet, which we'll put in the hotel safe. I will give you a formal receipt for it, and this you must hide away somewhere on your person. Are you listening? Good! You then go off to Innsbruck with the receipt, leaving the real packet with me, and the dummy in the safe. If your . . . friends . . . get you, and things get too hot, you will reluctantly produce the receipt from the hiding place. If they do come to collect, I shall know you're in trouble, because I'm the only one who has a key of the safe. In that case, I will then hand them the dummy packet and take what action I think necessary to reach you."

"What happens if I get to Innsbruck unmolested?"

"You put up at a hotel and telephone me. Then I bring the real packet along. I can do Innsbruck from here in a couple of hours. How's that for a plan?"

"It's good," said Jake, "but it's not on. I'm not having you involved to that extent. Wouldn't be fair."

"Cilli? What rot. Anyway, that's what we'll do, so stop arguing." His chin came out. Jake remembered the gesture of old, and knew protest was useless. Besides, an ally like Nicco was just what he needed.

"Oh well," he capitulated, "probably not much risk now. We've had plenty of shooting already, and somebody must have got hurt. To busy licking their wounds, I expect."

"Sure you weren't followed this morning?"

"Dead sure." He spoke confidently, but he had a niggling feeling that he could have been more vigilant. He brushed the thought aside. "The plan's perfect," he said. "The sooner I get going, the better."

"You're not going tonight. On that I insist. A few hours won't make any difference. You leave in the morning, old boy."

A small clock on the mantelpiece had struck midnight before their preparations for the next day were completed. Nicco had collected paper and string and, being methodical, had even found some waterproof material and a stick of sealing-wax. "Nothing less than an exact replica will do," he said firmly. When the job was done to their satisfaction, the dummy was locked in the safe, and Nicco took charge of the real packet. "Don't worry," he said. "I've got a private wall-safe in my room." When the receipt had been typed on hotel paper for "one sealed packet", Jake took off his shoe and stuffed it in the hollow heel. "One of Gostoli's efforts," he grinned.

Drinks were now produced to toast the success of the plan, and at last, yawning and stretching themselves, they drained their glasses. "Can you find your way to your room?" asked Nicco at the foot of the stairs.

"Sure."

"O.K. then. I'll see you're knocked-up about eight. Sleep well. There's nothing to worry about now; everything's organised. Goo'night."

Tired, but well satisfied with the night's work, Jake climbed to the first floor, strolled along the dimly lit landing and, turning the key, entered the room and switched on the light. He took a step forward and, too late, saw a movement reflected in the mirror opposite. The cry died in his throat as, turning, the full force of the blow caught him above the temple. He pitched forward across the bed.

TWELVE

Two men were talking. He could hear their whispered voices penetrating his deadened senses. He tried to say something, to cry out for help, but his mouth was constricted. He could feel something filling it, something nauseating and tasting of stale tobacco. His head throbbed abominably and his limbs felt rigid. Unable to move, he imagined he was boxed up in a narrow coffin. As he came up from the depths the whispered voices got louder and, consciousness returning, he caught the words "He's coming to. You got that gag fixed tight?" Then, at his side, another voice, "Yes, Boss."

Jake opened his eyes. He was in the hotel bedroom, lying on the bed, and there, at the foot, was 'The Boss', his ugly face twisted into a grin. Jake knew now why speech was impossible, why his limbs were rigid. A pad of evil-smelling rag filled his mouth, kept in position by a tightly-bound gag, whilst his legs and arms were tied with nylon cord. Their eyes met.

"You make no trouble," mumbled 'The Boss' in a low voice, "and you won't get hurt."

Jake turned his eyes. Poxy gave a grin, his yellow face puckering. "We got you now," he taunted. "Trussed up good. You've had rope enough." He chuckled, appreciating his own wit.

"Chuck it, Poxy—we got work to do. Get moving."

The smile left the little man's face instantly. With a

quick movement he raised Jake to a sitting position, then pulled his legs off the bed so that his feet were touching the floor. 'The Boss' came round to assist. "You're going out through the window," he said. "You make no trouble, everything'll be O.K.—otherwise . . ." He held up a piece of metal piping and waved it threateningly. Jake knew what had hit him!

His head ached unmercifully, and he could feel his temple throbbing : taking the guts out of him. The disappointment of it weighed heavily—he'd not reckoned they'd strike again so quickly. He watched in a detached manner as Poxy produced more cord and tied it round the leg of the big old-fashioned bedstead. When they'd tied the other end round his waist, knotting it carefully, they switched off the light and pulled back the curtains. As they carried him towards the window he caught a glimpse of the starlit sky and felt the cool night air on his face. They lifted him clear of the window-sill, and the next moment he was hanging in mid-air. It was a strange sensation : unable to move his limbs, he swung gently from side to side, his inert body now and again banging against the wall of the building. Presently he felt himself being lowered, and saw the stonework—not inches away—moving slowly past his eyes. The cool air revived him. He remembered the packet, and the receipt for the dummy hidden away in his heel. He smiled—maybe he'd outwit them yet!

When his feet touched the ground they held the rope taut. As he swayed gently, he looked around at his surroundings. He was in what seemed to be a deserted yard. In the distance he could hear young voices—revellers, perhaps, returning from a party. He tried to cry out, but Poxy had done his work well, and nothing escaped but a feeble moan. Then he felt the rope tremble and, looking up, saw Poxy climbing from the window. As soon as the little fellow reached the ground, he whipped out a jack-knife and cut the cord round Jake's waist. Almost at once 'The Boss' was at their side. He stood for a moment listening, then, apparently satisfied, rounded on Poxy. "Get on with it," he barked *sotto voce* : "Cut the rope round his feet, and give me the knife."

As the cord fell from his ankles, Jake felt his arm gripped fiercely by a huge hand. "Walk," said 'The Boss', his face close. The blade of the jack-knife flashed silver in the moonlight. "Walk," he repeated, "unless you want this between the shoulder-blades."

They came out into a back street where, a few yards away, stood a car. It was the blue Citroen Jake had seen near the coppice the previous night. Poxy opened the rear door, and the big man gave Jake a savage push which sent him sprawling across the seat, then climbed in beside him. With Poxy at the wheel, the car glided silently away, and was soon speeding through a labyrinth of narrow streets. How long the drive lasted, Jake had no idea, nor, at this moment, did he care. His head was throbbing damnably, and the gag over his mouth had opened up the wound Grogan had inflicted. He could feel the blood seeping again. He lost track of time.

Presently the Citroen slowed. He peered from the window and was surprised to see they were still in the town. He was bundled out and hustled across a narrow pavement and through a dilapidated door. He had time to see they were in a poor area, and that the house they were entering was shuttered and seemed unoccupied. He heard the squeal of the rusty hinges as they shut the door after him; then Poxy, armed with a torch, led the way up a flight of rickety stairs. Jake could hear the boards creaking as he climbed, and once he stumbled, almost putting his foot through a hole in the rotting woodwork. The whole place reeked of dry-rot. At the top Poxy went into a room, and presently they heard the scrape of a match and the splutter of a lighted candle. By the flickering light Jake had his first view of the sordid garret. Apart from an iron bedstead with a palliasse upon it, the room was without furniture. Near a shuttered window stood some upturned boxes, and in one corner there was an improvised bed of straw. It looked as if it had been used as a doss-house by vagrants.

Striding across the room, his body huge in the meagre space, 'The Boss' slammed the door with a savage kick. "Now then," he said, turning towards Jake. "Start talking." He nodded at Poxy, who untied the gag and took the pad from his mouth. Jake did some quick thinking. He knew what they wanted, but wondered to what extremes they'd go to get it. He knew, too, that if things got desperate he could always produce the receipt. But it would never do to capitulate too easily: that way they might suspect. . . .

"Start talking," repeated 'The Boss' truculently. "And don't think shouting'll do any good. There ain't no one in these parts who'll help."

"Talk? What about?" Anything to gain time. It would be hours before Nicco missed him. And then what?

"You know . . . the goods," shouted 'The Boss'. "The hot stuff."

"You must be joking."

"Don't act daft," the man spluttered. "You got the stuff, and I mean to have it . . . so hand over."

"I don't know . . ." 'The Boss's' hand came up. It landed where Grogan had already done so much damage. Jake fell back, wincing, feeling the blood spurt.

"I tell you, I don't . . ." he cried again, but 'The Boss' cut him short. The blow—with clenched fist—landing above the stomach, winded him, and he sank to the floor. He wondered how much more he could take—or, indeed, need take—before he gave in.

"Pick the bastard up, Poxy. We ain't begun yet."

Jake felt the little man's arms around him, and he was slumped on one of the boxes, his hands still pinioned behind his back. Then a great hand came under his chin, and his head was jerked up. He met the furious gaze of the irate man. "Listen, you," he growled. "I'm warning you for the last time—come clean—or else! It'll be like those buggers in the wood last night . . . same thing'll happen to you."

Jake gritted his teeth. Here was a chance of a diversion. "What happened to them?" he asked weakly.

"They got . . ." It was Poxy's voice.

"Shut your bleeding trap, you," screeched 'The Boss', raising a fist. Poxy backed away, fear in his eyes.

The face above Jake broke into an ugly smile. "You'd like to know, wouldn't you? Well, we ain't telling, see. But you can take it from me, it weren't good for their health."

"Thanks for nothing."

It was when the inquisition began again that Jake blundered. "I haven't got the damned packet . . ." he exploded. He stopped instantly, but 'The Boss' was on to it.

"The packet?" he cried. "Who said anything about a packet?"

Before Jake could reply, the giant had seized him by the ear. Though his hands were still tied behind his back, his legs were free. If he could but land one blow, to gain a short respite, he might reach the street. He saw the great hulking body barely a foot away. Forcing his aching muscles into action, he brought his knee up and sent it crashing into 'The Boss's' most vital parts. The man sprang back, doubled up. "You bastard," he screamed, beside himself with pain.

Rejuvenated by his success, Jake leapt to the door. Unable to use his hands, there was only one thing to do. He aimed a blow at the rotten timber with his foot. He heard the wood split, and stood back to rush it. But, with a tackle worthy of a Rugby player, Poxy dived at his ankles and brought him to the floor. He struggled to rise, but when he felt a huge knee in the small of his back, pinning him down, he knew his success had been short lived.

"Bind his feet, Poxy," gasped 'The Boss'.

Jake heard the patter of Poxy's feet as he fetched more rope. Then he was quickly trussed up and made to sit on one of the boxes. 'The Boss' slumped on to another box opposite and, glaring malevolently, said in a subdued voice, "Search him, Poxy; give him a proper frisking." The examination was lengthy, but at last it was done. "No good," said Poxy. " 'Tisn't there . . . certain sure of it."

'The Boss' roused himself : in the flickering light his face looked ghastly. "No more time to waste," he muttered. "Bring the candle, Poxy."

As Jake watched them straighten his legs and start unlacing one of his shoes, he realised their intentions. So this was it : torture ! Well, he couldn't stand for that—not for Gostoli or anybody. The time had come when he must talk : tell them about the receipt.

The big man was talking again. "A nice bright flame," he gloated, "between the heel and the ball of the foot . . . sure way to make obstinate buggers talk." He had Jake's shoe in his hand, and was twisting it around : examining it with crafty eyes. "Wait," he cried suddenly. "There's something funny here." Grasping the heel in his great hands, he gave it a wrench. A whoop of triumph burst from his lips as it yielded to the sudden twist, and the smile came back into his face. With clumsy fingers he pulled out the folded paper, and straightened it on his knee. Slowly the significance of it penetrated, and he looked up.

"So," he drawled, "that's the idea, is it? Afraid to carry the goods about with you, eh? Turning to Poxy, he pointed to the paper. "See this . . . this is a receipt . . . for the goods. The stuff's back at the hotel." He produced a heavy silver watch and flipped it open. "Yes," he ruminated, "in about . . . seven hours' time, Poxy, you'll be paying them another visit."

"That won't help you," muttered Jake. "They won't give it him."

'The Boss' gave him a withering look. "Pencil and paper, Poxy," he ordered. "You'll find both in the car—get moving." The little man flew from the room. Soon there was a flurry of footsteps, and he was back, the pencil and paper in his hand.

The big man turned his attention to Jake. "You've given

us enough bloody trouble already, but from now on you'll do as I say."

"And what if I don't?"

Jake saw the candle held up. "Right between the ball of the foot and the heel," chuckled the giant. "Now write," he ordered. "Tell 'em to hand it over to bearer. And no hidden messages, 'cos it won't work—see?"

"Tell me the exact words, then."

It didn't take long. There were just three lines of it, addressed to the manager of the hotel, directing him to hand the sealed parcel—receipt enclosed—to the bearer, a trusted servant! When it was done, Poxy came in for some instruction. "In the morning," he was told, threateningly, "you'll take the car to the hotel and deliver this note. If they ask any questions, tell 'em you know nothing—only that you've been sent for it. Say Mr Standish is too busy to come himself. And, if you value your life, don't you come back without it." He looked at his watch again. "Almost three," he muttered. "Let's get some sleep." Then he crossed to the iron bedstead and flung himself on to the palliasse. He turned on his side. "Kip down by the door, Chinaman," he muttered sleepily, "in case anyone starts sleep-walking." A scowl appeared on Poxy's face: he loathed these nicknames. How often he'd been tempted to rebel—stick a knife in the bully's ribs.

Watching Poxy, Jake saw him take most of the straw from the corner to make a bed for himself. Then the little man grasped him under the armpits, dragged him across the room, and laid him on the almost-bare boards. "We not untie the ropes," he said softly. "Too dangerous." He then put his mouth close to Jake's ear and whispered in a not unfriendly tone, "Make no shouting, or Hudson will put the gag back." So the big fellow was called Hudson! He'd learned something—not that it helped.

After a time it became sheer torture lying on his back, unable to move hand or foot. The excitement that had kept him going had long died—to be replaced by a black depression. The pain from his wounds gave him no respite. He sighed, wondering what would happen when Nicco discovered they'd got him : what he'd do when Poxy arrived to claim the package. The candle was burning low, and presently it gave a splutter and expired. It was dark now, a blackness more intense than he'd ever known—not a chink of light penetrated the shuttered window. He grew angry with himself : angry that he'd voluntarily embarked on this foolhardy enterprise.

Then he heard the rats! A faint scuttling at first, then the flitter of tiny feet across his legs. . . . He shuddered, closing his eyes. God! What next?

THIRTEEN

NICCO BULLIVANT was in high spirits. Calling to his wife,
"Just going to give Jake a knock-up," he took the stairs
two at a time. How great it was to see the old devil after
all these years! Still the same old Jake—always getting into
scrapes and somehow, with astonishing luck, getting out of
them! But this time he'd gotten himself a problem: something more than a mere prank. And what a turn-up that
his car should break down near Ulm! And of all the hotels
to choose The Laurent! Another of Jake's lucky strokes—
doubtful if he'd have handled the affair on his own.

When he reached the door of Jake's room he gave it a
hard thump. "Come on, laddie," he cried loudly. "Time to
show a leg." Getting no reply, he dived into his pocket for
his master-key, and opened the door. "Rise and shine . . ."
he began. The words died on his lips as, striding into the
room, he saw that it was empty. His eyes strayed to the
open window—saw the nylon rope leading away out over
the window-sill. He was across the room in a moment. The
rope reached to the ground. He knew there was only one
explanation: someone had struck first!

Sweating slightly, he gave the room a hurried run-over.
Not a clue. He saw the bed had not been slept in. So!
They'd got him as he entered the room. He looked at the
bed again. Someone had lain on it—the white coverlet was
crumpled and awry. Then he saw them, and his heart
turned over—bloodstains: bloodstains at the head of the
bed. Jake wounded!

Nicco's mind raced. What should he do? Phone the *Politzei*; tell them the truth? That would mean the whole story coming out. Jake wouldn't want that. Yet what was the alternative?

Nicco crossed to the window again. They'd obviously used a car—taken him off that way. Perhaps someone might have heard something during the night : seen the car, even. He grew calmer, thinking of their plan; remembering the receipt Jake was carrying. Of course! That was his passport to safety. Jake was all right. If things got too hot he'd hand over the receipt. What then? Presumably they'd come for the packet. Nicco wondered. . . . Better get down to the office anyway, he thought. He hauled up the rope into the room, closed the window, and slammed the self-locking door behind him.

Cilli was at her desk, briefing the receptionist. He called her aside. "Don't get excited, old girl," he whispered, "but I'm afraid we've had visitors during the night."

"What do you mean?" Cilli's eyes dilated.

"Jake's gone," he said quietly.

"He can't have. . . ."

" 'Fraid so. They got into his room last night. He's been kidnapped, abducted—call it what you will."

Cilli's eyes opened wider. "I knew he'd come to no good getting mixed up with that business."

"No good thinking about that now; it's too late."

"Well, there's only one thing to do, Nicco. You must get on to the *Politzei* right away."

"Not so fast." Nicco kept his voice low. "They must have got him soon after midnight, about eight hours ago. . . ."

"You must do *something*," broke in Cilli. "You'll just have to phone the *Politzei*, though I hate the idea of them prowling around. The guests will wonder . . ." Her voice tailed off.

"I'll make a few enquiries first, to see . . ." He stopped suddenly. A man had come in through the swing-door and was approaching the reception desk. Something about his

appearance gripped Nicco's attention; his nondescript
clothes, the shifty eyes, the yellow pock-marked face. As
Nicco gave the door a gentle push, so that he was hidden
from view, his eyes rested upon an attractive girl on the far
side of the vestibule, thumbing through a magazine. Waiting for someone, I suppose, he mused. He caught Cilli's eye,
and raised a finger to his lips. "Listen," he whispered.

Through the half-open door they heard the receptionist
wish the man *"Morgen!"*, but the fellow's reply was
drowned by the noise from a passing car. As the rumble
died away they heard the girl say, "If you'll wait, I'll see."

"What is it, Gretchen?" asked Cilli, as the girl came
into the office, a slip of paper in her hand.

"He says he is from Herr Standish. He gave me this . . .
says he's to have the parcel he left here."

Nicco stiffened. So it had happened . . . quicker even
than he'd expected. He kept his head, realising at once
what he must do. Turning to his wife, he said quietly, "You
must do exactly as I say, Cilli. Jake's in danger. Go and
ask the chap why Mr Standish cannot come himself. Ask
him where he is and, most important of all, find out if the
little man's come by car. Then come back to me—pretend
you're getting the parcel."

Cilli nodded. He watched her pass through the door. The
suspense was agonising. He could hear the murmur of their
voices : then, louder, "Wait here—I'll get it from the
safe."

The forced smile was still on her face when she returned.
"He says Jake's engaged on urgent business . . . will explain
when he returns tonight . . . must have the packet," she
whispered breathlessly.

"Yes, yes—but did he come by car? Did you ask him
that?"

"Yes, he's got a car. Said Jake was out of town."

"Right. Give him the stuff." Cilli raised her eyebrows.
"Yes, that's right. Give him the packet," he went on.
"Make him sign a receipt . . . anything . . . only, whatever

you do, keep him occupied a minute or two. I must have time . . ."

"What are you going to do?" There was anxiety in her face."

"Don't worry. Do as I say."

"Right."

Keeping clear of the door, Nicco crossed to the window. There was a car outside the hotel : a blue Citroen. Jake said something about a Citroen! Yes—it must be. . . . He slipped back to his desk. Cilli was at the safe, her back to him. "Keep the keys," he murmured as he felt round in the drawer and, finding an old Mauser revolver, stuffed it hurriedly into his jacket pocket. The thing had lain there for years : quite useless, really—no ammunition. Still . . .

Noiselessly he slipped out by the other door of the office, and was quickly in the street. The car was still there. Pray to God the idiot hadn't locked it! He crossed leisurely towards it and, with no more than a perfunctory backward glance, opened the rear door and got inside. Closing it quietly behind him, he looked back towards the hotel entrance. The man was still inside; everything, so far, was under control. He lowered himself quickly to the floor, covering himself with a coat he'd found on the back seat. Then, clutching the Mauser and crouching as low as possible, he settled himself to await events.

Cilli had done her work well. It was almost five minutes before he heard the door in front open, followed by a movement in the driving-seat. Then the starter whirred, and the Citroen glided away. Nicco supposed he was in the right car; it had been the only one outside the hotel. He cautiously lifted the edge of the coat and raised his head. Yes—there was no mistaking the stringy neck, the close-cropped hair. This was the car. He was on his way.

The drive seemed an eternity. Yet in reality it lasted no more than five minutes. Presently the brakes went on and the car stopped. Now . . . would the fellow look back?

Would he want the coat? Nicco waited—tense, ready for anything. He felt the pressure on the back of the driving-seat ease, heard the door slam, then the patter of running feet, dying away. He lifted his head in time to see the man slip in through the door of a house opposite. He did not look back. Though Nicco had not been in this street before, he had a fair idea of his whereabouts. This was on the outskirts of the town, where a few bomb-damaged properties still awaited demolition. He looked across at the house into which Poxy had disappeared. Obviously, the place was derelict—unlived in. He looked through the windscreen, then through the rear window—not a soul in sight! With a final peep at the house, he climbed from the car and, crossing the pavement noiselessly, reached the comparative shelter of the wall of the building. Pressed tight against the wall, he stood for a moment listening : then he slipped round to the back through a narrow alley.

He found himself in a small yard—indescribably filthy —beyond which was the river. The water looked menacing and evil. His thoughts ran away with him. A body—well weighted—could rot away : might never be found. Jake's words came back to him. "I bar getting bumped off and dumped in the river. . . ." Nicco shook himself; this was no time for getting morbid.

Turning his back on the river, he saw the house had a back door : it was off its hinges. This was a relief—surprise was his strongest weapon. He entered the house and moved slowly along the darkened passage, feeling his way carefully until he came to a flight of stairs. Looking up, he could see a light coming from a room above. Then every nerve in his body froze.

"Well then," said a gruff voice, "if you've got it, hand the bloody thing over, and quick about it." There was no reply, but a moment later the voice went on, "Good. Now all we got to do is to get it to Munich . . . to a certain gentleman—one of your sodding breed." There was another pause. Then, "See here, Poxy, this little trinket's worth a fortune. Neither you nor me is allowed to open it . . . it's got to go to you-know-who."

Listening carefully, Nicco caught the whispered reply, "Yes, Boss."

"I'm taking it. See!" The voice took on a truculent tone. "While I'm gone 'His Nibs' stays tied up. Understand? We ain't taking any chances with the likes of him, 'cos this little parcel might not be all it should be. When you been in the business as long as me you don't trust no one. So just you guard 'His Nibs' with your life, Savvy?"

"Yes, Hudson."

"So I should hope. Now where'd you leave the car?"

"Outside."

"*Outside?* You bleedin' whipper-snapper," roared Hudson. "I told you to leave it away from here. Now, if somebody's followed . . ."

"I'm tired of being . . ." began the thin voice of Poxy. But before the sentence ended Nicco saw the door of the upper room burst open and the little man come staggering backwards across the landing. "No! No! Not that!" he cried, as Hudson leapt at him.

"I'll teach you," yelled Hudson, seizing him.

With a hand on either side of the stringy neck, Hudson lifted the little man up until his head almost touched the ceiling, then, with a sudden sickening twist, flung him into the corner, where he lay huddled up. Crossing to the corner and lashing out with his foot, the bully cried, "Get up, you bastard. You ain't hurt." Slowly, with his hands holding his neck, Poxy got to his feet and stood cowering, fear in his face. But Hudson had not finished. "I . . . told . . . you . . . never . . . to leave . . . the car . . . outside," he roared. And to the utterance of each word his fist crashed into Poxy's head and face. Even before he'd finished, Nicco could see the blood streaming. Powerless to help, he saw the little man stagger into the room out of sight. Then he heard Hudson say, "I'm going now. Shan't be many hours. When I'm gone, you see to it that the door stays locked. It ain't

much use, but don't you open it to anyone. You got a gun
. . . use it, if necessary. And don't let Standish try any
tricks."

Nicco heard the hurried footsteps inside the room, then
the door slammed and the key grated in the lock. The
landing was dark now, but already Nicco had moved
quietly from the foot of the stairs and was crouching low,
beneath the banisters. His heartbeats quickened as he heard
the first of Hudson's heavy footsteps on the stairs. Slowly,
inexorably, they came nearer. When the man reached the
ground he stood for a moment, accustoming himself to the
half-light. To Nicco, crouched behind him, the huge bulk
seemed to fill the passage. There must be no half-measures,
he thought anxiously, otherwise . . . He raised his arm, and
with a sudden movement sprang forward and brought the
butt of the Mauser down on to the bare head with all his
strength. Hudson didn't even grunt : he just sank slowly to
the floor and lay still. Nicco took a deep breath.

His first reaction was one of relief. Relief that it had
been so easy, so silent. He listened a moment and smiled;
no sound came from the upstairs room. Going through
Hudson's pockets, he quickly found what he was looking
for. Having relieved him of his gun, it began to seem that
the situation was in hand. Yet already the disadvantage of
having no preconceived plan was becoming apparent. He
knew now, of course, that Jake was in the room above, but
he daren't leave Hudson. If only there were a place where
he could lock him up while he tackled Poxy. He glanced
about him, peering through the gloom, but no such place
existed. He frowned, wondering how to entice Poxy down
the stairs. Bending over the inert body on the floor, he
dragged it clear of the staircase. So this was 'The Boss'.
What an apparition! But even as Nicco gazed down at the
snarling countenance, the man gave a moan and opened
his eyes. They fixed upon his adversary : a look at once
malevolent and full of cunning.

"Not a sound," whispered Nicco, "if you value your life."

As he spoke he pointed the gun with a steady hand. "Your gun," he taunted, "and loaded—I made sure of that."

Hudson made no move, but Nicco was taking no chances. It was as he gazed at the man's crafty features that a plan —crazy, perhaps—suddenly came to him. "If you make one squeak," he said, "it'll be your last—*savvy*?" Hudson's eyes opened wide, giving him a puzzled look, for the words were uttered in a voice that might have been his own!

Nicco gave a soft chuckle. Impersonations! It was years since he'd done any—but it was worth a try. . . .

Pointing the gun threateningly at Hudson, he shouted, "Poxy! Poxy! Come quick—*quick*." The impersonation of the voice was perfect—the pitch, the tone, the bullying resonance of it. Hudson gasped, pop-eyed.

The effect was electric. From the room above came an answering cry of "Coming, Boss," then the door on the landing opened and Poxy appeared. Slowly, as if every move was agony, he began feeling his way down the stairs. "Coming, Boss," he cried again breathlessly. He was almost in a state of collapse when he reached the ground floor.

"Drop the gun, or you're a dead man."

For a moment Poxy stood looking utterly bewildered, then his legs gave way beneath him and he crumpled to the floor in a dead faint. Nicco, triumphant now, raised his voice, crying, "Nicco here, Jake . . . be with you in a minute." Hudson, still dazed by the turn of events, was given a kick in the ribs and told to "Get up, you great bully, or you'll get plugged." A moment later he was on his feet. "Now pick up Poxy," ordered Nicco, "and get up the stairs. . . . *Move*." A minute later all three were in the upstairs room.

Jake was lying on some straw, bound and gagged. Gazing down at the still figure, Nicco's anger rose; he wondered if he was too late. He glanced back at Hudson, who had dumped Poxy on the floor, where he lay huddled, his face ashen. "If anything's happened to my friend," he bellowed, "I'll . . ." He turned, hearing a rustle of straw, and saw

Jake's eyes open : fixing him a dog-weary stare.

One-handed, it was an almost impossible task to free him from his bonds. Nicco dare not take his eyes off Hudson, nor dare he enlist his help. But at last it was done. "Are you all right, old fellow?" he asked anxiously.

Jake sat up and moved painfully. "Been here, trussed up, all night," he grunted. "Be O.K. presently."

"Try standing up," urged Nicco. "Walk about a bit. I'll deal with Hudson later." Hudson shifted his gaze to the door, as if measuring the distance.

Nicco raised the gun. "I wouldn't try it," he muttered grimly.

It was slow work getting Jake back into something like shape after his ordeal, but at last he managed to stand up, and presently to walk a few steps. To begin with it was sheer hell, but gradually his deadened limbs came back to life. The cut over his temple and at the side of his mouth still ached, and he complained of a pain in the head. But though there was a tenderness above his stomach, the blow from Hudson had done no real damage. When at last his vigour returned, the questions came. Did Poxy come to the hotel? Did Nicco guess what had happened? How did he find his way here? Though they glanced occasionally at Hudson, they did not notice he'd moved perceptibly nearer the door.

"Shouldn't we be getting these fellows roped up?" asked Jake presently.

But Nicco was too flushed with success. "We'll tie 'em up in a minute," he said.

There was a momentary silence, and it was then that Hudson caught the faint sound outside which sent a wave of hope through him. It was as if someone was creeping up the stairs. The others could not have heard it, because Nicco was talking again—boasting. He pointed a derisory finger at Hudson. "You must hear how I fooled him. Just listen, Jake, and I'll give you a sample of the fellow's voice." He threw back his head, and with a realistic imper-

D

sonation cried out loudly, "At last you're at my mercy—
I am going to kill you."

The laughter died on their lips, for as the words fell away
the door flew open and Nella, a tiny silvered revolver in
her hand, burst into the room.

"Nella!" shouted Jake.

Quick as light, Hudson jumped. Only one step was
needed. In a flash a great arm encircled Nella, and a huge
hand wrenched the gun from her fingers. He wasted no
time. Using the girl as a shield, he backed towards the door.
"Come, Poxy," he cried. Then, shifting his glance, he
screeched, "If you bastards move, I shoot." He looked again
at Poxy, a huddled form on the bare boards. "Are you
coming?" he cried angrily.

The Chinaman rolled on his side, turning a pair of
frightened eyes towards him. "I can't," he cried. "I'm
done."

What followed was too terrible to contemplate. For
Hudson, his mouth set, raised the gun and pressed the
trigger. They heard the scream of the bullet, saw the blood
spatter, and watched Poxy sink back to the floor.

"You won't talk now, you bastard," muttered Hudson,
backing through the door and slamming it after him.

In silence they listened to the heavy footsteps as, taking
Nella with him, he clumped down the staircase.

FOURTEEN

JAKE was the first to recover his composure. "Don't say it, Nicco," he urged. "You weren't to know." Rousing himself, he cried, "Quick. Get down to the street . . . see if he's gone."

Glad of the diversion, Nicco dashed for the stairs. He was quickly back. "He's gone," he muttered despondently. "I just saw the Citroen rounding the corner—the girl was with him."

"What happens now?"

"The packet's no good to him, anyway," replied Nicco. "It's only a dummy."

"Damn the packet," flared Jake. "Who the hell cares? He's got Nella . . . that's what matters. Good God, man —anything may happen."

"Nella? The girl you told me about. I saw her in the hotel, watching . . . must have followed me."

Jake covered his face with his hands. "Oh, God! What'll Hudson do with her? What can we do, Nicco?. . ." His voice died away. It was only now the bare truth hit him: that he realised what she meant to him. Oh, Nella, he thought, what have we done?

From the corner came a croak. "Poxy!" they cried together. They turned towards the prostrate figure and, kneeling, pillowed his head with some straw. That the man was alive was a miracle. The bullet had passed through his neck and buried itself somewhere in the woodwork. Blood was everywhere. A pair of staring eyes gazed up at them. It was obvious the man had not long to live.

"Quick," said Jake, bending closer. "Tell us . . . tell us where he's gone." But Poxy, his eyes already glassy, seemed beyond comprehension.

"Quick," urged Jake, cradling him in his arms. "Hudson's a killer . . . see what he's done to you . . . he'll do the same to the girl. Tell us—*where has he gone*?" The bloodstained lips opened: he was fighting for words. But no reply came.

"Will he have gone to Munich, perhaps?" prompted Nicco, remembering Hudson's words.

Though the staring eyes did not move, there was an imperceptible gesture of assent.

"The address, man, the address? We promise to get him . . . to get revenge for you."

The ghost of a smile crept into the grey face, and the dying man's lips twitched. Then he croaked the single word "Ching", and fell back exhausted. It seemed he'd gone. But he'd not finished. Again the lips moved, and in a final desperate effort he gasped, "*Wellingstrasse* . . ."

"*Wellingstrasse*?" echoed Nicco. "Must be the name of a street."

"Maybe," murmured Jake, looking up. He felt a sudden twitch, and the frail body in his arms went limp. When he looked back, Poxy was dead.

"Poor devil," he sighed.

"What'll we do with him?"

"Leave him here," said Jake, lowering the corpse to the boards. "He's past help. It's Nella we've got to worry about. If anything happens to her . . ."

"We've got to get after Hudson." There was urgency in Nicco's voice now. "It's our only chance."

"Munich?"

"Obviously . . . a street called *Wellingstrasse*."

Jake gave a gesture of despair. "Hopeless," he muttered. "Probably a mile long."

Nicco stood for a moment, deep in thought. "Ching?" he ruminated. "I wonder what he meant by that?" Then he gave a laugh. "Of course," he shouted.

"What?"

"Don't you remember Hudson's words, or were you too far gone? Said he was going to Munich . . . to give the packet to you-know-who—*one of your sodding breed*. Poxy was Chinese; anyone could see that. What we've got to do is to find a Chinese called Ching . . . somewhere in the *Wellingstrasse*."

"It's possible."

"It's a bloody cert."

"But how?" groaned Jake. "How the hell can we follow?"

Nicco was thinking; wondering how much time they'd lose getting back to the hotel for his car. Then, "Nella's car," shouted Jake, hope in his voice. "She must have come here by car. To the street, man, quick!"

With astonishing agility for one who'd gone through so much, he raced for the stairs. As he ran through the passage his foot kicked against something. "Poxy's gun," explained Nicco, as they ran out into the street. "Glad you stopped to pick it up. Always useful."

Out on the pavement, they glanced in both directions. Surely it must be? They'd pinned such faith on it! Desperately they looked again, first up the street, then down. Then Jake saw it. "Look!" It was a cry of triumph. "Right at the end of the road. . . . I'd know it anywhere."

Nicco got there first, and was already looking inside. "Bless the girl," he said, "she's left the key in the ignition. Damned careless—but what a bit of luck!"

The sun was high overhead as they swung into Munich. Though it was his first visit, Jake was too preoccupied to take any interest in the gleaming buildings and fine modern shops through which they were passing.

At a traffic block Nicco explained that, though he'd never heard of the *Wellingstrasse*, he knew Munich fairly well because his sister-in-law, Sonya Mittlefelt, lived in a villa outside the city. He and Cilli had often stayed there. "Her husband, Adolph," he said, "does something in chemicals; research, experimental work. But Sonya—she's a great girl. You'll like her."

When they stopped to make enquiries Jake caught the word *Wellingstrasse*, but otherwise the conversation in German was lost on him. "What did he say?" he asked as they drove on.

"Five minutes from here."

After a short drive along a wide street, they turned off. Then, passing through a maze of busy streets, they reached a comparatively quiet locality. Here ancient and modern buildings mingled incongruously together. Looking up, Jake caught a glimpse of a sign, "*Wellingstrasse*". They had arrived. A few yards away they came to a turning marked "*Parkenplatz*" : the policeman, so Nicco said, had told him there was a car park handy.

"There's one bit of luck," said Jake as he climbed from the car. "It's only a short street. Shouldn't take long to give it the once-over."

But Nicco was for caution. "Far better," he said, "to get Sonya to spy out the land for us. If you go blundering down the street you might get recognised . . . that is, if Hudson has come this way."

"I suppose you're right. Perhaps we'd do better . . ." He stopped suddenly, his heart thumping crazily. "Look, Nicco," he gasped, pointing a finger. "Look . . . the car . . ."

"What do you mean? What car?"

"Hudson's car . . . the Citroen!"

It was true. Not twenty yards away, at the other side of the car park, was the blue Citroen. There was no mistaking it—they'd both been taken for a ride in it! Nicco raced across and put a hand on the radiator. "It's still warm," he said. "He can't have been here long—now what do we do?"

"Every minute's precious now. I don't care what you

say, Nicco—I'm going down that street. Might find out something."

"I think you're crazy. If Hudson should see you, God knows what'll happen."

"I'm going anyway. Wait here."

The *Wellingstrasse* was no more than a couple of hundred yards long. It was a narrow street, bounded on either side mainly by small shops and stores. There were a few people about; the odd shopper with a basket over her arm. Leaving the car park, Jake crossed to the shady side and strolled along the pavement. Though trying to appear casual, his eyes roved everywhere: to the windows on the opposite side—through any open door—up any passageway—probing. Success came quicker than he'd expected. He had covered no more than half the street when he saw the sign. His heart lurched: this must be the place, must be the man. He stopped, rooted to the spot, gazing. On the other side of the street, above the ground-floor window, he read:

HUNG CHING, CHINESE RESTAURANT.

His first thought was of Nella. Somewhere in this building she was a prisoner, unless Hudson had cast her adrift *en route*. He remembered what had happened to Poxy, and his imagination started conjuring up every kind of gruesome fate for her. Gazing across the narrow street, it suddenly came home to him just how powerless he and Nicco were to go to her assistance. Could they find an excuse for entering the restaurant? They could, of course, go in as customers, but what good would that do? As he stood back in a doorway, pondering, he could see their only chance of success was to postpone their operations until nightfall. But would it then be too late? What might happen in the intervening hours? Clearly, Nicco must be consulted. But first he must get a mental picture of the place, so they could make their plans accordingly. As an artist he had trained himself to observe, and during the next few minutes hardly any relevant detail of the scene before him escaped his notice.

It was a 16th-century building, in a poor state of repair, with its rotting window-frames and peeling paintwork. But there was one significant feature which caught his attention: the shutters of the small attic window were closed. Could it be? He smiled grimly, wondering. From the front only one door, leading into the restaurant, was visible. He would have liked to explore the rear of the building, but had tarried long enough.

As he moved off to return to the car park he made what seemed a vital discovery. Two houses distant from the restaurant some demolition was in progress. The whole of one building had been removed, and those on either side shored up with timber. Though the foundations of the new building were already laid, it was the space at the rear which caught his attention and set him thinking. For a moment he was unwise enough to stop and gaze across at this space, noting with satisfaction the conglomerate of building material and equipment of every kind—including ladders. The discovery brought a smile to his face: here— if they had to wait for darkness—was at least one way of getting into an upstairs room! He moved hurriedly up the street, well content. But had he looked back he might have noticed a flutter of the curtains in the window above the restaurant. Some sudden draught in the room, maybe?

"You've been a hell of a time," Nicco greeted him. "You had me worried."

Trying to sound calm, Jake leant across and whispered, "I've found Ching's."

Nicco sat up. "You what?"

"Found Ching's. It's a Chinese restaurant, just down the street. It's called Hung Ching." He pointed towards a corner of the car park. "The back of the place is somewhere over there."

Nicco frowned. "Hung Ching? Could be. . . ."

"Must be," said Jake emphatically, as he got into the

car beside him. Talking rapidly, he described the building, mentioned the demolition work and told him of the ladders. "There's nothing for it," he ended, "but to wait for darkness. It's hell, but it's the only way."

"There's still something else we can do."

"What's that?"

"Telephone Sonya," replied Nicco.

Darkness closed in early. It was just before sundown that great black clouds came rolling in, darkening the sky and bringing with them the threat of heavy rain. Sitting in Nella's car, the gloom surrounding them, Jake stretched. "Soon be able to make a start, Nicco—no point in waiting until the rain starts."

"And no point in being too precipitate. We've been lucky so far . . . mustn't spoil it."

Jake's patience was wafer-thin. How the time had dragged. It wasn't as if he'd spent all of it in the car, either. How grateful he'd been for those few hours' sleep at Sonya Mittlefelt's. Now, sitting in the car beside Nicco, waiting for the moment to arrive, he pondered on the events of the last few hours. First, Nicco's excitement when, coming back from the telephone, he'd announced that Sonya insisted on helping them. "She's coming here right away," he grinned.

Jake had taken to her at once. She had charmed him by her friendly and warm personality. After some argument Sonya insisted on going off to Hung Ching's to see what she could find out. There had been an anxious half-hour while she was away, as Nicco had had some misgivings about bringing her into the affair at all. "God knows what Mittlefelt would say if he knew," was his comment. But at last they saw her hurrying back into the parking-place.

"I had a snack," she had told them, in passible English. "No one took any notice—I was just another customer. Then I had a real break." She grinned, pleased with her English slang.

"What happened?"

"A young man came in," Sonya continued, "and asked to see Herr Ching; wanted to make enquiries about a wedding party."

"Well?"

"It's their reply that is so important," she explained. "They said Ching was away and wouldn't be back until midnight or later. Don't you see?" she cried. "If he's away until midnight, you've got lots of time. You told me yourself, Nicco, that the man Hudson must give the packet to Ching personally. And if the girl really is there, surely Hudson would never do anything to her without consulting his chief?"

Sonya's words, "if the girl really is there", had, to Jake, an ominous ring. All their plans were based on the assumption that Nella was actually in the house. Maybe she never even got there! Back came the doubts, the morbid thoughts. Perhaps she'd already been cast aside; some lonely woodland glade; some foaming torrent. He shuddered. "Probably too late, anyway," he said despondently. "I expect Hudson caught Ching before he left."

"Nonsense," interrupted Sonya. "They said he left early this morning—don't forget that. So stop worrying, Jake. You'll have plenty of time to put your ladder up after dark, and rescue the girl before Ching gets back."

It was after this that they prevailed upon him to go to Sonya's for some food and sleep. And how he'd slept: more than four hours of deep, strength-reviving slumber. Meanwhile, Nicco had been obliged to remain in the car park to keep an eye on Hudson's car. While Jake slept, Sonya returned to the car park, where she and Nicco had an earnest and crucial conversation. Before she left she put something in Nicco's hand. "Remember," she said, "it is not a toy."

The evening was well advanced by the time Jake got back to the car, and since then time had dragged. It was Nicco who broke the long silence. "We should be able to move off soon," he said. Then, "When you left Sonya, did she give you a torch?"

Jake felt in his pocket and produced it. He brought out something else and held it up. "Poxy's gun," he muttered.

"Good lad," observed Nicco. "Now have a look at this." Without a word of explanation he took from his pocket a small cardboard box, similar to a fountain-pen box but not as long. He removed the cover and thrust the box across. At first Jake could see nothing inside, then, looking closer, he saw what seemed to be a white pencil resting in a layer of cotton-wool.

"What's so marvellous about this?" he asked. "What do we want a pencil for?"

"That's no pencil. Careful!" he warned. "The thing's lethal . . . well . . . that's not quite true."

"What's the mystery? If it's not a pencil, what is it?"

"Take it easy, old chap, and listen. Sonya, who's got her head well stuck on, thinks we're taking a hell of a risk, bursting in on Ching's. She believes even the worst could happen—and I'm prepared to go along with that."

"We're armed."

"Guns. Yes, I know. But remember, once we're inside every hand will be against us."

"It's a risk we must take."

"Not without additional precautions."

"How do you mean?"

"You remember my telling you that Adolph, her husband, is some sort of chemist, experimental, and all that. . . ."

"Yes."

"Well, apparently he's recently discovered a new drug— a type of 'knock-out' drug—which acts instantaneously, though only effective for a short time. It leaves no harmful after-effects. It's top secret, but Sonya thinks it's to do with crime prevention—a project he's working on. Adolph's away on a lecture tour, and as some of this drug has been put into the special injectors he's invented, she's whipped one for us. This is it : but it's only to be used if we get into a real jam."

"Do you mean this pencil thing contains 'knock-out' drops?"

"Sure thing."

"This is all very well, but a chap like Hudson isn't going to oblige by baring his arm so you can give him a hypodermic."

"That's the remarkable thing. This stuff is effective wherever it enters the body—a mere prick of the skin will do it." Nicco removed the 'pencil' from its box and held it up to what was left of the light. He pointed to the tapered end. "See that?" he said. "Hidden in there is the needle. The moment the point is pressed on the skin a spring operates, and . . . bang . . . the deed is done."

"You must be joking."

"On the contrary. Sonya swears it works—and I believe her. If we get cornered, well . . . it's a comforting thing to have around."

It sounded improbable to Jake. Nevertheless, he stuffed it in his pocket, and again looked at the sky. Must be dark enough now, he thought.

It was as they were preparing to move off that he first saw the light. It came from a window high up in one of the houses backing on to the car park. He sat upright. "That light," he said excitedly, "I haven't noticed it before. It's from Ching's—or very near it." Together they peered through the windscreen, trying to pinpoint its exact position. "That's the house," said Jake shakily. "I know it . . . it must be Ching's." As he spoke, the light went out. "Blast," he muttered. "It might have helped." But suddenly the light came on again and started flashing—on and off. What the hell was it playing at? Fascinated, they gazed at it : at first uncomprehending. But then : "It's a signal," yelled Jake. "Look, Nicco. . . ." Spellbound, they watched the square of light spell out its message : . . . — — — . . .

"It's Nella! I knew it . . . she's in that bloody attic. She's signalling for help. Quick, Nicco, if you've got a heart."

"But how could she possibly know we're here?"

"Doesn't. Wants to attract attention . . . anyone's attention."

They watched a moment longer. Then, slowly, unmistakably, it came again : . . . — — — . . . Twice more the signal came, then it ended. But the light stayed on. They saw it as a beacon, guiding them. . . .

FIFTEEN

"Come on," cried Jake. "There's no time to waste—every minute's precious."

"I know, I know. But for God's sake keep calm. You'll get nowhere if you start blundering. . . ."

"Well, come on then."

Keeping within the shadow of the few remaining cars in the park, Jake led the way towards the wall at the far end. They moved silently: each fitted out with a pair of Adolph's rubber-soled shoes! Sonya had also provided Jake with a dark pullover that blended well with the gloom of the night. Every detail of their plan had been worked out with painstaking care, and they both knew that, provided they could find a long enough ladder, nothing could stop them getting up to that attic window. Even if it rained, then with their rubber-soled shoes they would succeed. Now that the moment for action had at last arrived, Jake's fears and doubts evaporated. *En avant!*

In a dozen yards they had reached the wall. The reflected glow in the sky from the brightly-lit city shed a vague lustre on the blackness around them. From this glimmer of light they spotted a heap of stones. They climbed this, and raised their heads above the coping. Below, vague and shadowy, lay the demolition site, and beyond—some twenty yards distant—the foundations and pygmy stonework of the new building.

"Then Ching's must be the next but one," said Nicco in a whisper.

Leaving the pile of stones, they moved to the far end of

the wall, where it turned away at right angles. Here it was all of seven feet high. "Give us a leg up," said Jake. Nicco cupped his hands to receive Jake's foot, and a moment later whipped him aloft. Resting his elbows on the top of the wall, Jake saw he was but a few yards from the kitchen of the restaurant. This was at once apparent from the piquant smell of cooking coming from a door at the rear. A huge window at one side of the kitchens gave on to a small area, spilling its brilliance out into the surrounding darkness. From the bustling shadows that passed and repassed this stream of light, and from the excited jabbering inside, it was obvious that Ching's was doing a good business at this time of night. Their visitation was well timed!

Looking upward, his eyes traversed the tall building, moving slowly from storey to storey. It was as they had thought—the same height at the rear as in front. Even in the unlikely event of their finding a ladder high enough to scale this obstacle, the chances were that it would be too unwieldy to handle by themselves: certainly with any degree of silence. It was as well they had done their homework—as well they had realised this difficulty—for as soon as Jake shifted his gaze to the adjoining building he saw that they'd planned wisely. The important thing was that although this structure was of similar height to Ching's— three storeys and an attic—it differed inasmuch as it was T-shaped; the wing which projected towards the car park, and doubtless an addition to the old house, being, as they had already noticed, only two storeys high. Furthermore, this wing was so constructed that the apex of its roof abutted on the *bottom edge of the roof of the main building*. Jake reckoned it would not be difficult to find a ladder capable of reaching the lower roof. Once there, it should be relatively easy to work their way up on to the other, and thence across to Ching's and up to the attic window. What pleased him was that both roofs were edged with an eighteen-inch parapet. A comforting thought!

"Lower away," said Jake, realising from the movement of Nicco's shoulders that he was getting impatient. "I've seen enough. It's all clear."

"Come on, then let's get the ladder."

Moving softly in their rubber-soled shoes, they were soon in the plot of the demolished building. They moved back and forth, searching. It was growing even darker: black clouds scurried across the sky, and the wind was rising. They daren't use the torch too freely, but at last its beam lit upon something metallic—it was a lightweight metal ladder, and it looked the right length. It was easy enough to pass it from one to the other over the wall separating the two properties. They were now in the yard of the house adjoining Ching's. Jake put a cautioning finger to his lips, and for a moment they stood in silence, listening. Apparently all was well so far: they'd neither been seen nor heard. From Ching's came the excited jabbering and shouting of a busy kitchen staff. This was music to their ears! As they stood listening, they gazed up at the dark, silent house before them. There were only two windows—one on each floor—and both were closed and in darkness.

Working quickly, they raised the ladder into an upright position, and then allowed it to come to rest gently against the building. They peered upward, seeking to penetrate the gloom.

"I should think it's high enough," murmured Jake. "Let me shin up first. When I'm O.K. I'll give the ladder a tap —then you follow." Nicco nodded approval.

Dead easy, this part, thought Jake, as he went up, counting the rungs. Ten more left, he guessed. Five more rungs had gone, and his hands reached the top. Straddling the parapet, he pulled out Poxy's gun and struck the ladder a sharp tap. From the shadows below came an answering tap. Then he felt the tremble of the ladder as the rungs were climbed. Next, Nicco's curly head came up out of the darkness. "Piece of cake so far," he said, grinning. But Jake was already on the move, creeping carefully along behind the parapet towards the wall of the main building. Here, with the wall at one side to steady them, it would be easier to work themselves up to the top of the lower roof.

"Come on, Nicco. We've not got much time. Rain's starting."

Above them the dark clouds had now closed in, and already scattered raindrops whipped their faces. In five minutes the scud would be a deluge.

Reaching the wall, Jake dropped on all-fours and began to climb the roof. The instant he lifted his knee under him and found his shoe gripped the wet tiles, his spirits rose. Without Adolph's 'rubber-soled' it might have been hopeless. As it was, it was difficult enough, for, although his feet were gripping, it was almost impossible to find a hand-hold. By fumbling around he found a cracked tile, and hanging on with two fingers managed to pull himself up an arm's length. It was painfully slow. First the groping round in the dark, then at last a chipped or broken tile, then a gain of perhaps a foot. Then suddenly the storm erupted. The skies opened, and within seconds the rain had turned the roof into a raging torrent. Hanging on by little more than a finger-hold, Jake sought desperately to maintain his position. He had almost reached the apex of the roof and, though the rain almost blinded him, could see the ridge-tiles a yard above him. He stretched an arm to reach for the top, but the movement upset his equilibrium, and his foot slipped. . . . He flung his arms wide, vainly attempting to clutch at anything that might save him, and with a muttered curse came sliding down over the tiles. He ended up against the parapet: angry, sweating and drenched to the skin.

"You all right?" This from Nicco, another shadowy, rain-sodden figure.

"Bloody cross," was the reply. "I had the top within my grasp." Jake shook the wet from his eyes in an impatient movement. "It's like a skating-rink already."

"We'll never do it that way now. Tell me—how far to the top do you make it?"

"What? You mean . . . up to the ridge-tiles?"

"Yep."

"About fourteen or fifteen feet, I should think."

"All right, then. We can do it easily. Can't think why it didn't occur to us before."

Nicco's plan needed little explanation. "Do what I say," he cried above the screech of the wind. He got to his knees, then, rolling over on to his back, braced his feet against the parapet. In this position his shoulders were resting some five feet up the slope of the roof. It took Jake little enough time, with a helping hand, to scramble up alongside him and get a foot on each shoulder. Using a hand to keep the rain from his eyes, he glanced upwards. His head was still some five feet from the top. He felt Nicco's hands gripping his feet, then came a heave, and up he went, almost a yard. He reached out his hands and—Eureka!—his fingers gripped the ridge-tiles. He had made it! Below, Nicco felt the pressure on his hands ease. "I'm there," he heard Jake's exultant cry.

The really tricky part was to come. For now Jake had to hold on to the ridge-tiles while Nicco, using his friend's legs and body for support, climbed up beside him. Even now it was touch and go, for although he had a powerful grip on the apex of the roof, the tiles were slippery, and the pull on his hands and arms terrific. But at last Nicco, grinning with delight, straddled the roof-top.

"Get moving," said Jake relentlessly. "We've lost too much time already. Remember, we've still got to get down again . . . with Nella." Then, straddling, he quickly jerked his way to the adjoining roof. This part was not difficult, and they were soon safely behind the parapet, ready to move round to the attic window. Leaning over, they glanced down. Below them, at the back of the building, everything looked normal : no sudden switching-on of lights, no sudden cry of alarm. Mercifully, the rain was easing. Jake felt a glow of contentment, for now he was almost there. One more corner to round, one more roof to scale: and then Nella! Now, with rescue only minutes away, his excitement was almost overpowering.

Feeling their way cautiously along the edge of the roof, using the parapet as a guide—daren't use the torch now—they reached the corner of the building and made a right-angled turn. They were there! Jake looked up. There above him, not ten feet away, was the attic window—its light burning brightly. He turned and pointed a finger. "Same procedure," he whispered, "but not a sound, mind."

Nicco braced himself against the parapet, and as soon as Jake was above him and in position, he pushed. He waited, and presently the weight on his shoulders eased as the climber took hold of the window-sill. There was a momentary silence as he awaited the order to move. . . .

"Oh, Nicco, Nicco!" It was a cry of anguish.

He turned and, looking up, saw Jake's face—dead white —pressed against the window pane, grief etched in every contour.

"Quick, Nicco, for God's sake!" Jake, gripping the sill, leant down to give him a hand, and the next moment they were side by side, clinging desperately to the rotting framework of the window. They looked in through the dirty glass to the lighted room.

It was a sight never to be effaced from Jake's memory. The tragedy of it—the hell—the anguish—it was like a knife twisting in his bowels. For there, a crumpled heap on the faded floor covering—the shining revolver clutched in her outstretched hand—was Nella! Nella, an inert figure, still as death, her face to the wall, her dark hair tousled.

SIXTEEN

"OH, NICCO," groaned Jake, tight-lipped. "She's shot herself. Why—oh why?" A white-hot anger gripped him, and he raised a fist to send it crashing through the window.

"Easy, old boy," said Nicco. "It may not be as bad as it looks." There was a soothing quality about it that restrained him. The quiet voice went on—"No need to break the glass. The wood's rotten; if we push hard enough the catch'll go through it—less noisy."

They put a hand to the window frame and gave it a thump. With a sharp crack of splintering wood, the catch burst through the rotten timber, and the window swung inwards. "Nella! Nella!" cried Jake. "It's Jake."

But from the huddled mass on the floor came no movement. Within the room all was still. Outside, where they clung with tiring fingers, the storm had quietened, and here, too, was a stillness broken only by faint whisperings round the chimney-stacks. Jake gave a harrowing glance at his companion, as of a man suddenly bereaved. Then, without speaking, he grasped the top of the dormer and, doubling up his legs, swung them over the sill and dropped noiselessly to the attic floor.

"Got your gun?" asked Nicco softly, swinging his legs inward.

Jake held it up for him to see, then, moving lithely across the room, dropped to his knees at Nella's side. He put the gun on the floor and, with infinite tenderness, placed his hands on her shoulders and turned her towards him. . . .

The next moment a pair of almond-shaped eyes were blinking up at him as, with a sudden movement, the girl swept his gun away and covered him with Nella's revolver. It was like some crazy dream. Instead of Nella, this was a Chinese girl dressed in her clothes. At a glance he could see venom written in every wrinkle of her sallow face. Yet his first reaction was one of relief. Thank God it was not Nella! He stood up, his thoughts on her: wondering. . . . As he did so, a shadow crossed the wall, and Hudson, the inevitable automatic in one hand and an eighteen-inch carving-knife in the other, stepped from behind a screen.

"If at first . . ." he chanted, his face split in a hideous grin.

It was only then that the full realisation of the trap came home to Jake: no wonder the man was jubilant. Yet how could Hudson have known? He must have seen something to make him suspect. What pleasure he must have had, getting the girl to dress up in Nella's clothes. Jake swept these thoughts aside; being bested by Hudson mattered little compared with his anxiety for Nella. What had they done with her? Since they'd taken her clothes, the chances were that she was still in the building. His reverie was interrupted. Hudson, confident now, was wise-cracking. "Miss Ching," he explained, waving his hand. "A small-time actress, playing her first important role. Not bad, was it?"

He caught the expression on Jake's face, saw his knuckles showing white as his fists clenched. "Not advised," he warned, a mocking grin about his ugly mouth. "I shoot well, but I'm deadly with this." He held up the carving-knife, its long, narrow blade catching the light—glinting murderously. "Used to be a butcher before I took up this sort of work," he explained.

"And what sort of work might that be?" enquired Nicco, finding his voice.

"Ah!" replied Hudson knowingly. Then abruptly the mood changed. Gone now was the smile, the bantering tone. "You young fools," he shouted, leaning forward belligerently. "You'd have come to no harm if you'd given up this morning—cut your losses. But no, you had to meddle with what don't concern you, and follow me here. So it's going to be curtains for you—tonight. Now! Ching don't encourage trespassers."

"Get on with it, then," cut in the Chinese girl tartly. "My father will be back soon; he'll not wish to be bothered with trifles. Shoot, and be done with it."

It became clear to Jake then that if there was to be any hope of escape or success they must act before Ching returned. . . . Yet Hudson was in no mood to be hurried, for, throwing out his massive chest, he announced proudly, "You don't easily outwit Hudson, you know. I knew exactly what you'd do." Then he laughed again, and went on, "The signal was a masterly stroke. . . . I knew it would fetch you." He stopped, and as an afterthought asked: "This address? How did you get it? Poxy? Is that it?"

"Yes. He lived long enough to tell us that much."

"The little rat! Never could be trusted. Told lies as well. Probably lied about your bandy-legged friend."

Jake pricked up his ears. Grogan! Perhaps now he'd learn what happened. "What did he do to . . . my bandy-legged friend, then?"

Hudson grunted. "Might as well tell you . . . make no difference now. Poxy shot him: plumb through the head. Leastways, that's what he said."

"And what about the other—the one you plugged . . .?"

"For Christ's sake!" screamed Miss Ching, her lips taut, Nella's .22 in her hand. "Cut out the time-wasting. Shoot now, Hudson, or I'll do it for you."

"I wouldn't do that," advised Jake coldly. "If you kill us there'll be nobody to tell you where the real packet is hidden." He shifted his gaze to Hudson, and with a smile added, "You see, the one you've got is a dummy—quite valueless." He had realised, ever since the trap was sprung, that Nicco and he were safe enough until Hudson laid hands on the genuine article. But it wasn't their own safety he was worried about—it was Nella. Somehow she had to be found : somehow they had to outwit Hudson and this murderous Chinese girl. It was as he shifted his stance that he felt the slight pressure of 'the pencil' against his leg; until that moment he hadn't given the thing another thought. Just another of Nicco's wild ideas, was how he summed it up. But now, up against it as they were, anything was worth a try.

"What was that you said?" faltered Hudson, his blue stubble-covered jaw dropping.

"I said it would be unwise to kill us . . . no one left to tell you where the real packet is."

"I don't believe it." The pitch of his voice told Jake that the shot had gone home. He shrugged his shoulders. "That's up to you. But if you don't believe me, why don't you open it?"

Badly shaken, Hudson glanced nervously in the direction of the girl. She turned on him like a viper. "If you've balled it up . . ." she hissed.

"It can't be . . ." His face had gone green.

"Better not be. You know what he does to failures."

"But all hell will be let loose if he finds I've opened it."

"Sure. And if he opens it and finds a dud?" She raised an arm and ran a finger across her throat. "That's what," she added crisply.

"What'll I do?"

"Stop dithering, and open the bloody thing."

"Take my gun, then."

"One's enough," was the tart reply. Her eyes caught Jake's as he watched Hudson push his gun into his jacket pocket. "I'll knock you both off if you try," she cautioned.

Hudson was busy at the table. At last, the final wrapper unfolded, he stood gazing incredulously, his mouth agape. Then the truth registered, and the knowledge that he had been fooled sent his blood coursing. "You double-crossing bastards," he screamed, lunging forward, his huge arms flailing. "You'll pay for this."

"Hudson!" The girl's voice, the lash of a whip in it, stopped him instantly. "Cut out the rough stuff," she blazed. "Time enough for that if they won't tell you where the real goods are . . . and if you haven't got them when *he* returns, God help you."

Hudson looked a broken man. Suddenly all the bounce and swagger had gone out of him, leaving only a gaunt giant across whose features had crept an expression of abject fear. It was evident that Ching dealt summarily with bunglers. As Jake lounged impassively against the table he could feel the friendly shape of 'the pencil' again. Things were moving his way! Soon the time would come to test its powers. He knew now that this was their only chance : he must risk all, and put his trust in Adolph. "The lady talks sense, Hudson," he said. "Rough stuff won't help you. You want the packet—I want the girl. I'm prepared to make a deal." Out of the corner of his eyes he saw Nicco's startled look.

"Well?" said Hudson, brightening.

"If I tell you where it is, do we—that is, my friend and I *and the girl*—get set free?"

"And if I did agree? You'd lead me up the garden more'n likely."

"No. You can keep us here until you've collected it. I'll trust you to keep to the bargain." Nicco's face was a picture. Jake shot him a reassuring look.

Hudson could hardly believe his ears. The grin came back to his face. He could collect the parcel, and eliminate them afterwards. Dead easy !

But the Chinese girl wasn't foxed so easily. "A likely story," she scoffed.

Jake gave her a withering look. "It's up to him. He's the one who wants the packet."

"Yes," she snapped, "and you're the ones who want the girl—and your lives, maybe?"

"We're safe enough. . . ."

"Unless we try, shall we say . . . a little persuasion."

"We're not worried. No time for that. Hudson needs that packet, and quickly." Jake stopped and, looking across at him, added, "You could collect it and be back here in a few minutes."

Hudson's eyes shone. "It's in Munich, then?"

"Sure."

"It's a deal. You tell me where it is, and as soon as I get back you'll be released."

"Where's the girl now?" asked Jake hopefully.

"Keep your trap shut, Hudson." This from Miss Ching.

Hudson frowned, gave a shrug of his massive shoulders, and muttered grudgingly, "She's around."

"Is she unharmed?"

"She ain't hurt."

Though he would have liked to pursue the matter, Jake guessed it would be unwise to try and make further conditions, especially with the Chinese girl so hostile. "All right," he said. "And you'll release all three of us?"

"Yes. All three." Hudson looked at his watch. "Christ!" he muttered, galvanised into action. "Quick—tell me where it is, so's I can get going."

"I'll need paper to draw you a rough plan—back of an envelope'll do." Jake kept the excitement from his voice. Would Hudson suspect? Would he co-operate? So much depended upon how he and the girl acted during the next minute. So much depended upon Adolph's magic, and whether Nicco, when he saw what was happening, would be quick enough to deal with the Chinese girl.

With anxious eyes he saw Hudson dig into a pocket and bring out a dirty envelope. Jake held out his left hand, and keeping his voice steady said, "That'll be all right. Let's have it, and I'll show you how to get there." As he brought his right hand from his pocket, he added, "I've got a pencil."

The move was so natural that Hudson, unsuspecting,

held out the envelope. His hand was now no more than a foot away. Jake reached out to take the paper, and as he did so his right hand came across and the pencil point struck. It was a good shot, landing on the ball of Hudson's thumb. . . .

The man sprang back, bellowing with rage. Sensing a trick, he rushed forward. As the great arms enfolded him, crushing the breath from his body, Jake heard a shot and saw Nicco drop. This must be the end! So this was what came of trusting to the new-fangled ideas of some crackpot chemist! At any moment his ribs must give under this murderous pressure. But even as he looked into the face in front of him, he saw the expression change. Then the encircling arms became flaccid, and Hudson's huge frame, like a dying elephant, sank slowly to the floor. *It had worked!* The miracle had happened—Hudson would give no more trouble for a while.

The noise of a scuffle behind him reminded him the battle was not yet over. He whipped round to see the Chinese girl struggling in Nicco's arms. Though he had a strait-jacket grip on her, and a hand over her mouth, she was lashing out with her heels and striving to get her teeth into his fingers. Jake didn't know then that when she fired at Nicco he'd been quick enough to drop to the floor, and before she'd had a chance of a second go, had whipped round and got a grip on her from behind.

"Grab her gun," cried Nicco, "in case anyone heard the shot. You'll find it on the floor somewhere. Then give me a hand with this hell-cat."

As Jake rounded the table and spotted the .22, his eyes lit on the 'pencil' lying close by. He must have dropped it in the excitement. Nicco's face brightened when he held it up for him to see. "Great work," he said. "Quick, give this blasted woman a shot."

Half a minute later Nicco was carrying the unconscious girl across the room, where he threw her on to the bed.

"You sure she's out?" asked Jake.

"She's out all right."

Jake crossed to the door. "You'd better collar Hudson's automatic. I'm going to find Nella. You stay put." He let himself out on to a dimly lit landing and, moving across to the banisters opposite, looked down. A flight of stairs led to a brightly lit landing below. He stood listening, astonished at the uncanny silence : with a restaurant on the ground floor it seemed impossible there should be no noise. He heaved a sigh of relief. In a place so well sound-proofed, they'd not have heard the shot.

Now all he had to do was to find Nella. All! Then he remembered the shuttered window in the apex of the gable. Of course! That must be it; otherwise, why the shutters? He turned. Sure enough, there was another door—locked. In a moment he was on his knees, with an eye to the key-hole, but he could see nothing. Then he remembered the shutters again. Of course, the room would be in darkness! Then he heard a sound, first a moan, then a creaking. "She's here, Nicco," he cried, his eyes alight. "Quick, bring Hudson's knife."

The waiting was intolerable, and before Nicco came Jake had charged the door. It was a flimsy affair and offered little resistance. At first he could see nothing but the blackness before him. He heard Nicco's voice—"The switch, you idiot," and on came the light. Then he saw her, and his heart leapt.

Clothed only in underwear, her mouth gagged, her eyes blinking across at him, she was roped to a chair, bound hand and foot. He raced across, and in a flash whipped the gag from her mouth and cut the ropes. Their eyes met and he reached down and lifted her to her feet. "Oh, Jake," she murmured. "You managed it." Then his arms were around her.

"Break it up," cried Nicco. "Time's running out. . . . The dope only lasts a quarter of an hour."

"My old friend Nicco," explained Jake with a shaky laugh, helping her towards the door. In the other room they passed the prostrate form of Hudson and came to the Chinese girl. Nella mouthed a question, but Jake, already tearing off the girl's shoes, cut her short. "Tell you later . . . time's short. Get into your clothes as fast as you can." Unceremoniously, he had the slacks and jumper off Miss Ching, and then Nella was ready. With a final look at the unconscious girl, and a muttered "She's O.K. Out cold," he grabbed Nella's hand and raced for the window. Nicco, who'd been by the door keeping watch, was there before them.

"Blast and hell," he cried, "it's started again." As he spoke there was a crash of thunder overhead, then the rain, a torrent, splashed on the roof outside. "Damned luck," he went on. "Still, we can't wait—Hudson'll be round any moment."

"You go first, Nicco. I'll send Nella down as soon as you reach the parapet." The girl's eyes rounded as he spoke, but she said nothing. "It's all right," he explained. "It's all organised—you'll be quite safe."

They watched Nicco swing himself up and squeeze through the small window. Outside, he gripped the sill and lowered himself until only his head was showing. "Get Nella up after me, and for God's sake hurry," he said. Then he was gone. Standing on tiptoe and looking down, they saw him, a dim shape, already by the parapet.

Turning to the girl, Jake said, "There's nothing to worry about, darling." His voice had a note of anxiety.

"I'll be O.K. I've a good head for heights. Just give me a leg up."

He picked her up bodily and passed her—feet first—through the window. "Grab the sill," he ordered. "Turn face down, let go and slide—Nicco's at the bottom."

Whispering " 'Bye," she let go. He could hear the scrape of the tiles as she slipped downwards. He looked out and, seeing her safe by the parapet, called, "Quick, Nicco, get moving so there's room for me down there." Then he was in the window.

Something, intuition maybe, made him look back. Hudson, like a man waking from a deep sleep, was sitting up, rubbing his eyes with the back of his hands. Catching sight of Jake, he stopped suddenly, then, bellowing like a bull, he heaved himself to his feet and lurched towards the window. Jake grabbed the window-frame and turned. As he did so, it gave a sickening heave. Desperate now, Hudson threw himself up into the window space and flung his arms forward in a last despairing effort to stop him. Instinctively, Jake let go of the sill, and felt himself sliding backwards over the tiles. Then he was safe against the parapet.

He looked up and, horror struck, saw the dormer come hurtling towards him. It went past, missing him by inches. Through the blinding rain he saw Hudson, terror in his face, pitch forward, clawing the air, and spreadeagle outwards. He gave a terrified cry, barely audible against the background of the storm; then, as his head hit the parapet, the huge body somersaulted and disappeared over the edge.

SEVENTEEN

THE *Gasthof Unterberg* was small. But it was its undeniable charm that made Jake take it to his heart the moment he saw it. Perched on one side of the hill which winds up from Innsbruck to Igls, it seemed the embodiment of a typical Tyrolean villa, warm and welcoming. "So this is the place," murmured Jake to himself, finding it difficult to connect this enchanting corner of the Austrian Tyrol with the greasy Gostoli.

As he absent-mindedly switched off the engine and sat looking at the hotel, he remembered how Gostoli had made him repeat the words "*Gasthof Unterberg—Gasthof Unterberg*" over and over again, telling him on no account to commit the name to paper. He remembered, too, how he'd received the oft-repeated warning of secrecy, and how Gostoli had refused even to give him the name of the man he was to meet. It were better, he said, that Jake should not know the name of the purchaser—for what he didn't know he could not pass on—even under duress.

"What will I do, then, when I get to the hotel?" Jake had enquired. His instructions had been simple. All he had to do while staying at the *Gasthof* was to be sure that every morning between eleven and eleven-fifteen he was in the lounge, reading some English book or periodical. This fifteen-minute visit to the lounge was to continue each day until he was approached by a man who would greet him with the words: "Have you come from South America?"

When Jake laughed at this, Gostoli had gone on, "This is

a serious business, and don't forget you're doing very well out of it. You must follow my instructions carefully. When you are asked 'Have you come from South America?', you must answer 'Yes—from British Guiana!" Do you understand?"

Jake had grinned, but told Gostoli he could rely on him to carry out his instructions.

The 'toot toot' of the M.G. behind him reminded him that he was not alone. He flicked the Hillman into life and turned in through the gate of the *Gasthof*.

Looking back on it, and bearing in mind that she'd followed him to Ulm, it had seemed the obvious thing that she should accompany him for the rest of the journey. Yet how the three of them had argued about it. Nicco, curiously, had been all for Jake giving up the whole project. "After all," he'd said, "you've been damned lucky. What's more, but for Nella and me, you'd be dead twice over!" But in spite of all he'd said, Jake had insisted. What spurred him on he didn't know. He supposed it was because he'd said he'd get the packet through, and felt a certain obstinacy about it. Besides, what had he to fear now that Grogan and Hudson had been disposed of? Grogan? Well—if Poxy's word was anything to go on, there'd be no trouble from that quarter. And Hudson? The last he'd seen of him was lying face down amidst the fallen masonry with his head crushed beyond recognition. That well-timed clap of thunder, drowning the collapse of the dormer, had been an act of Providence!

During the drive to Sonya's, Nella had been singularly quiet. Jake mistakenly put this down to her recent experiences, but a few hours' captivity had bothered her little; she'd been in many worse situations. No, what was troubling her was what she was going to say when Jake started asking the inevitable questions. She needed time to think! After they'd eaten, she had done her utmost to avoid being alone with him, but the tactful Nicco made an excuse and took Sonya off to another room. The moment they'd gone, Jake was across the room and had his arms around her. She uttered a cry of happiness, and gave her lips to him. It was ecstasy.

For some minutes the only sound in the room was the steady 'tick tock' of the grandfather clock in the corner. At last she shook herself free. "Oh, Jake," she cried, anguish in her voice. "This must stop. . . . It's . . . it's just too . . . bloody."

His eyes widened. "Why, Nella . . . what on earth?"

"We can't go on like this."

"Why not? You know how I feel . . . and you can't be completely indifferent—you did follow me to Ulm, you know."

"That's got nothing at all to do with it," she answered dully.

"Oh." There was bitterness in his voice. "All right, then. What's the real reason?"

She was silent for a while. Then, slowly: "You were always getting into difficulties. . . . I wanted to be with you . . . in case."

"I don't believe you. There's something else."

"That's all I can tell you."

He took her by the shoulders, and looked into her eyes. "Tell me," he said earnestly. "Who are you? Why are my movements so important to you? Are you, too, working for Andre?"

"Andre?" she repeated. "Who's Andre?"

Was she lying? Her surprise seemed genuine. "Gostoli," he explained. "Andre Gostoli, the dealer."

She hesitated a moment. Then in a flat voice—"Oh . . . Gostoli!"

So he had been right; she was working for him. The resentment showed in his face. "I suppose he sent you to spy on me. Afraid I'd run off with his precious . . ."

"Oh, don't be so stupid," she burst in. "It's nothing of the kind. I didn't even say I knew him."

"But you do, don't you?"

She gave an emphatic "No," then slowly, as if picking her words, she went on: "I know of . . . your man, Gostoli, but I have never actually . . . met him."

"But you know about the packet . . . the stamp, or whatever it is I'm carrying?"

"I know a lot of things, Jake dear, but I can't talk about them. I can't tell you what I'm doing, or why: not yet, anyway. And when I do . . . you'll hate me. But, believe me, I'll do everything I can to prevent your getting hurt. So please, please, let me come with you to Innsbruck."

"Innsbruck!" The word shot from his lips. "How did you know?"

"Does it matter?" she said flatly. "Just do as I ask. I'll see you get the stamp there."

"I sometimes wonder if it is a stamp."

"It is, you know." She spoke with conviction.

"The whole thing seems so damned involved, just for a stamp." Frowning, he put her from him and began to pace the room. He turned suddenly. "I've a good mind to chuck it all. We both seem to have got into something that's doing neither of us any good. Perhaps if I chucked it, we could . . ." He broke off, alarmed at the expression on her face.

"No, no," she panicked. "You can't . . . you mustn't. No, no . . . please, Jake."

He crossed to her at once. "Why, Nella," he murmured, "you look positively scared."

She plucked nervously at his hand. "Please, Jake," she begged, "don't give up now. And listen . . . even if you gave up now, it wouldn't help . . . us."

"I don't understand."

"Don't try to, darling. Just do as I ask, *finish the job*. And let me come with you, I beg. I promise you it'll be for the best."

"Are you suggesting it might be dangerous to go on, because if so, that's a good enough reason for leaving you behind. You've done enough for me already."

E

"Please, Jake. . . ."

"Anyway, now we've got rid of Hudson and . . . the others, surely all danger is over?"

"Maybe it is; maybe it's just beginning," she answered cryptically.

"You talk in riddles, darling. First you think I'll hate you for what you're doing, then you want to come with me to protect me. I don't get it. . . ." Then Sonya and Nicco came back into the room.

Next morning, when they were returning to Ulm, Nicco gave him some advice. "Get back to Gostoli, old boy," he'd said, "and tell him what he can do with his blasted packet."

It was then that Nella had given Jake a sideways glance. Up to that moment he'd been indecisive, but now, meeting her eyes, his mind was suddenly made up. "Rubbish!" he said, vehemently. "I've started this thing, and I'm going to finish it. What's more, Nella's coming with me." Nicco was furious—even described Nella as an adventuress, and tempers flared. The temperature eventually cooled, and Nicco finally realised that further argument was a waste of time.

It was not until the next day that Jake and Nella, each in their own car, had left for Innsbruck. In spite of further protestations from Nicco, Jake insisted on taking the packet with him. "You've helped enough," he'd said. "And anyway, there'll be no more opposition."

It was when they were consulting Jake's Foreign Touring Guide together before leaving that Nella noticed someone had inked over a route with a ball-point pen. Curiosity made her turn the pages, and she found that a route all the way from Ostend to Innsbruck had been so marked. She looked up, incredulous. "Did you do that?" she enquired.

"Yep. I did it before I sailed. Did it without thinking. I'd forgotten all about it." He laughed, and pointed an accusing finger, "So that's how you knew where I was going!"

Her denial surprised him. "It was a damn fool thing to

do," she said. "Anyone interested, who'd been in your car, could have seen it." They thought no more of the incident for a couple of days. Then something occurred which brought the conversation into focus.

But now, as Jake turned into the drive of the *Gasthof Unterberg*, his immediate anxiety was whether so small a hotel could accommodate them both. He need not have worried. Herr Shultz, the proprietor, bland and red-faced, said this was no problem. A room had been reserved for Herr Standish, and as for the *Fraulein*, "charmed to oblige."

A few minutes after they went to their rooms something happened which disturbed Jake's peace of mind yet again. He was crossing the entrance hall to fetch his pipe from the car when he happened to glance back, and saw Nella at the telephone booth by the side of the staircase. Curious, he quickly retraced his steps. The booth, no more than a hood suspended from the wooden panelling of the staircase, was immediately below him when he stopped to listen.

"It'll happen any day," she was saying. "And do, please, stop nagging. I'll let you know where, just as soon as I can find out. I must go now . . ."

He slipped quietly up the stairs and back to his room. What the hell *was* she playing at? Who was she phoning? An idea occurred to him, and he went down again to the hall. Herr Shultz was at his desk. "By the way," said Jake casually, "did Miss St Clair pay for her telephone call, or would you like me to settle it now? Hardly worth entering on the account."

"She settled, thank you." The proprietor laughed, adding, "It was big enough to go on the *Rechnung*—Brussels is quite a long way!" So it was Brussels! Not that this was much help.

The two days which followed their arrival at the *Gasthof* were sheer bliss. They were both determined to shut from their minds all thought of the future, and live for the present. Even so, there were times when they became prey to their thoughts, and an awkward silence would develop to cloud their happiness. Jake did his daily chore faithfully. Punctually at eleven he would go to the lounge with a copy of the Continental *Daily Mail*, and stay there the requisite time. Though he made a pretence of reading, his eyes were always wandering towards the window and door in expectation. But for two mornings nothing happened.

On the first morning, after this chore had been done, they set off for a day in Nella's car. The weather could hardly have been kinder, and they motored leisurely from Innsbruck along winding roads until they reached the Fern Pass. Here they stopped to look at the lakes. Though small, their colouring was magnificent, and their setting perfect. The slender pines encircling the lakes threw deep shadows of unbelievable clarity across the unruffled surface of the green water. To the artist in Jake it was an enthralling spectacle. Nella, who had long since given up the pretence of being a painter, was equally appreciative. Near Ehrwald, the mighty Zugspitze towering high above them, they saw a track leading off the road towards the foothills. Here, leaving the car, they walked until the road was far behind them. A short climb brought them to a grassy plateau set in the side of the hill where, to one side, a tiny rill splashed and gurgled, clear and sparkling in the sunlight. It was a perfect setting for their alfresco lunch.

At length the meal came to an end, and they lay for a time side by side, smoking and alone with their thoughts. For a while neither spoke, but, though they were silent, both knew that sooner or later it was bound to happen. It was a chance remark which brought Jake to his elbow to gaze down at her as she lay enticingly near. "Oh, Nella," he murmured, "you're lovely." As he leaned over, she lifted her arms and came to him with a passion startling in its fierceness. At first her lips, then presently her body, yielded to his, and they became one. Now the world, and everything in it, was theirs.

When their passion was spent, they lay on their backs,

hands clasped, their minds content, their bodies at ease. "So you believe that one day I'll come to hate you," he murmured dreamily. "Nella darling, I could never hate you."

He felt her fingers tighten in his. "I wish I could believe it," she returned passionately.

The following day something happened to bring him quickly back to reality. Nella wanted to have her hair done, so after 11.15 they went off to spend a few hours in Innsbruck. They strolled happily down the *Maria Theresien Strasse* and, before Nella went off to the hairdresser's, agreed to meet outside the next-door café for lunch. Jake was quite content to roam around by himself, and was so interested in everything he saw that he had to hurry to get to the café on time. He need not have exerted himself; she wasn't there! Knowing visits to hairdressers are unpredictable, he was not unduly worried when, half an hour later, she'd still not arrived. But when he heard a clock chiming the next quarter, he began to get anxious. But a few minutes later he saw her running towards him, her face pink with exertion. "Quick, Jake," she cried, "into the café, then I'll tell you."

She refused to explain until they were seated at a table and the waitress had gone. Then, leaning towards him and lowering her voice, she said, "Guess what, Jake? I've seen him . . . at least, I'm almost certain it was . . ."

"My dear girl," broke in Jake. "It might help if you were a bit more coherent. Seen who?"

"Why . . . your bandy-legged friend, what's-his-name?"

"What! Grogan? Impossible!"

She nodded her head vigorously. "It must have been. Those legs—those long arms! Ugh."

EIGHTEEN

JAKE stared across the table at her. "Couldn't you have been mistaken?" he asked. "Poxy said he'd killed him, you know."

"Then Poxy must have lied," answered Nella. She went on quickly, "Anyway, forget Poxy and listen. I was not forty minutes late without cause."

"Go on."

"Well, I spotted him as soon as I came out of the hairdresser's. I'd finished there and was looking about to see if you were around, when I saw this figure walking into the hotel opposite. I'm pretty good at recognising people, so I whipped across the road and took a peek in through the open door."

"You took a big risk; he might have seen you."

"He'd only seen me once, remember, and then in a poor light."

"The light was just as poor for you: you might be mistaken. Anyway, go on. What happened next?"

"He was at the desk, but I was too far off to hear what he was saying. He was there only a moment, for as I looked I saw him give the receptionist a salute of thanks and turn away. As he came out I pretended to be interested in something in a shop window. I would have given a lot to go into the hotel and try to find out what he'd said, but instead I followed him down the street. I had no fixed plan in mind, but I knew the only thing to do was to keep going. My only worry was whether he'd run into you. But as he was walking away from this café I didn't think it very likely."

She broke off suddenly, and Jake looked up to see the waitress at their side. When the girl had gone, Nella went on to say how she'd continued to follow him almost to the end of the long street; but it wasn't until she saw him stop suddenly and dive in through the door of another hotel that she guessed the object of these visits. This time she waited partially concealed in a small arcade opposite. Within a few minutes he reappeared, and she watched while he stood at the entrance studying a small notebook before setting off down the street again.

"I knew you'd be desperate by now at my not turning up," went on Nella. "So instead of following him further, I crossed over and went into the hotel. By this time I had a fairly good idea of what was going on, so without any preamble I asked the young man at the desk if a Mr Standish was staying at the hotel. It was a long shot, but it worked. 'That's odd,' the fellow said. 'You're the second person who's asked that. Why, only a minute or two ago a gentleman was here asking the very same thing.' I enquired then if he was a stockily-built man in a dark suit, and he replied that it was. After that," continued Nella, "I went back to the other hotel, and found that Grogan had asked them the same question. Don't you see, Jake, he's guessed somehow that you're in Innsbruck, and he's going round the hotels."

"He'll have a job," laughed Jake, "and if he's going to comb the entire neighbourhood he'll be here . . . quite a while."

"I wouldn't be too optimistic, if I were you; this man's no fool. He may not be alone . . . could have someone doing a bit of telephoning."

"Yes. You're right—he's no fool."

"Well, my advice to us," said Nella briskly, "is to get back to the hotel this afternoon, and lie low until your other friend turns up."

"Sure you weren't spotted?" Jake seemed at last to have realised the importance of her discovery.

"Pretty sure. Anyway, he gave no indication that he'd seen me."

"He wouldn't. Grogan's crafty." Though he didn't know it at the time, Jake had never spoken a truer word!

It was soon after eleven next morning when the stranger came into the lounge. Jake was certain this was a newcomer to the hotel. He was a man of middle age, and everything about him spelled respectability, yet Jake was instantly suspicious. Another of Grogan's playmates? Glancing across to where Nella sat thumbing a woman's magazine, he caught her expression and knew she had the same idea. Fascinated, Jake watched him as he crossed to the window and began to roll a cigarette. What, he wondered, would be the fellow's next move?

Since his conversation with Nella in the café Jake's mind had become so obsessed with the probability of Grogan striking again that it came almost as a shock when the man turned suddenly and, walking across to him, whispered, "Have you come from South America?" It was unbelievable! He couldn't possibly be anything to do with Grogan now, for the test question had been kept a tightly guarded secret—not even Nicco or Nella had been told.

He recovered from his surprise. "Yes," he replied, "from British Guiana."

The man inclined his head. "That is good," he observed gravely; then went on, "I am Otto. As you know, I have come to take you to my employer." It was a strange accent, but the English was passable.

"It's all right," said Jake reassuringly, as he caught Otto's enquiring glance in Nella's direction. "She's a friend of mine. You can talk freely." Otto gave her a polite bow.

"Now," went on Jake in a crisp tone, "I want to clear up two points before we go any further. First, I want to know where we are going, and, secondly, I insist you tell me the name of your employer. I've been kept in the dark long enough."

Otto gave him a puzzled look. "In the dark?" he queried.

Jake made a gesture of impatience. "I mean, there's been far too much secrecy. You answer my questions, then I'll come with you."

"I regret, it is not possible. I am not permitted to say anything except to tell you that tonight, at midnight, I will call to drive you to my employer's . . . house." The hesitation over the last word did not escape notice : 'house' was a common enough word in any language! Curious!

"Of course, if I'm not to be trusted . . ." He broke off suddenly : Nella was shaking her head vigorously.

"Don't make difficulties, darling," she murmured lazily. "When we go with the man tonight we'll know soon enough where we're going, and who we're going to see. We must, of course, go with Otto when he calls."

Otto shot her a grateful look, but followed it with a shake of the head. "I apologise very much," he said in a precise manner, "but he must come alone. I am not permitted to take anyone else."

"Not permitted?" echoed Nella tartly. "Seems to me you're not permitted to do anything." This was going to upset all her plans. She gave a careless shrug of her shoulders, and went on languidly : "Oh well, I don't mind really . . . I just thought it would be company for you, Jake."

"The whole bloody outfit seems crazy to me," exploded Jake. "I've a good mind . . ."

"Don't be difficult, dear," said Nella, coming to his side. "Remember, you promised."

His ill-humour melted instantly. "Oh, all right. If that's the way you want it, there's nothing more to be said." Turning to Otto, he said, "Be here at midnight—I'll be ready."

For the first time a flicker of a smile crossed the man's face. "That is good," he said. "Dress warm," he added.

"The drive is long and the car is open." He turned and walked quickly from the lounge.

By the faint dashboard light Jake could just see the hands of his watch. They had already been on the road more than half an hour. Innsbruck was well behind them, and it seemed they were travelling roughly in an easterly direction. He knew little of the local geography, but the ribbon of creamy water which came into view intermittently suggested they were following the valley of the River Inn. He wondered if their destination could be Salzburg. Once or twice he had made an unsuccessful attempt to engage Otto in conversation, but soon gave this up, and, after satisfying himself once again that the package was in its proper place, he settled back and let things take their course.

Not so Nella! Ever since Otto had said she could not go with them she had been in a state, getting more steamed-up as the day wore on. "It's vital," she'd cried out once. "Absolutely vital that I should know where you're going." She became so agitated that when, ultimately, she came to him with a plan which seemed fantastic and quite unnecessary, he had promised to co-operate.

"I realise now," she said tremulously, "that you won't know where you're going until you actually reach your destination. What's more, when you do get there you won't be given the opportunity to tell me . . . or anyone else for that matter. Therefore we must do something about it."

She took a gilt powder-compact from her handbag. "Now, please, Jake, take me seriously, and listen. In here," she explained, "is some Austrian money—300 schillings— also a card. On the card is a message asking the finder to ring me here, and tell me where the compact was found. It also says that if the finder carries out these wishes a further reward will be paid." What Nella did not mention was that the message, in German, ended by pleading for prompt assistance as a man's life might be at stake. "All you've to do, Jake," she finished, "is to find a way to drop the thing secretly—as near to the damned house as possible—and leave the rest to me."

"Jake looked into her harassed face. "Wouldn't it be a good thing to come clean—tell me all?"

"Would to God it were possible."

"You know—with you getting in this state I'm wondering if I'm a B.F. to go. Perhaps it would be better . . ."

"No, Jake," she cried passionately. "Don't let's go over all that again, please." The girl seemed almost at breaking point.

"All right, darling," he soothed. "I'll go, of course. I'll do anything you want. I promise."

Lying back in the seat of the car, Jake remembered how —just before Otto arrived—she handed him a metal cigarette-case. "I've put some money, and another note, in this," she said, almost apologetically. "Please drop it, not too far from the compact. Just a precaution—mustn't put all our eggs in one basket."

When, promptly at midnight, Otto came, she seemed to take a grip on herself. She'd lit a cigarette, and with a casual wave of the hand had given him a breezy " 'Bye for now." But he wasn't so easily fooled: he knew just how much effort the restraint cost her. As he walked to the car with Otto he marvelled at the amount of 'ironmongery' he was carrying. In his hip pocket was the battered cigarette-case, and in his trousers pocket he had the powder-compact and, on her special instructions, her .22 revolver. "You have it," she'd insisted. "It's much lighter than that great thing of Poxy's."

As they left the hotel and drove off, neither Jake nor Otto was aware that another car, parked some distance away, had begun to move in the same direction. At this particular moment the following car was without lights, so there was every excuse for their ignorance.

Motoring through the night with the taciturn Otto, Jake subconsciously watched the beam of the headlights as they unfolded the white road before them, and now and again revealed some sleepy village. After they'd passed through a sizeable unidentified town, it became apparent that they had branched off on to a secondary road. For now there seemed to be a complete absence of other cars, whilst the road itself had become narrower and more winding and hilly.

Eventually Jake dozed off, but suddenly, through his slumbers, came Otto's voice, loud and urgent. "Quick, rouse yourself. We're being followed."

Waking instantly, Jake turned in his seat and looked back. It was some time before he saw it, but at last he caught the flicker of lights some distance away. "Yes," he said. "It's a car all right. What makes you think it's following us?"

"While you slept I kept changing speed, but it was always the same distance away."

"That doesn't prove . . ."

"It is following," interrupted Otto doggedly. "Your lady friend?" he asked suspiciously. "She wouldn't be playing tricks, would she?"

Jake felt a tightening in his throat: the thought hadn't occurred to him till then. "You need not worry about her," he told Otto. "She'll have gone to bed hours ago." Yet even as he said it he wondered. . . . Might not the compact, and everything that went with it, be just one great bluff? With Nella, anything was possible.

"I trust you're right, for her sake," observed Otto cryptically.

They had just turned a corner when Jake felt the brakes slammed on. The car slowed to a crawl. "We'll soon find out," said Otto, leaning forward and taking something from the shelf below the dashboard.

Following the beam of the headlights, Jake saw they were at the top of a long, straight hill bounded by thick pine woods. They had not covered more than a couple of hundred yards when the lights of the following car swept into sight.

Then everything happened!

One moment the car was rounding the corner; the next, its headlights suddenly blazing, it was thundering down upon them, closing the gap at breakneck speed. Fascinated, he saw the car—a big Mercedes—pull out, and with a rush of wind sweep up alongside. Then suddenly the lunatic driver, apparently bent on edging them off the road, swerved violently to the right.

"*Mein Gott*," screeched Otto, tugging at the wheel.

Now all Bedlam broke loose as, with a scream of tyres and a sickening scrunch of grinding metal, the two cars, locked together, zig-zagged down the hill. Then, with a mighty effort, Otto disentangled the tourer, and it swung to the right. Jake saw the Mercedes leap forward and swerve away in the opposite direction. He watched it, out of control, spin a complete circle, and in a beam of light caught the agonised expression on the driver's face as he clawed at the useless steering wheel. As the car charged into the trees and disappeared from view, Jake knew that Nella had not been mistaken. The driver was Grogan! Yet even as his brain got the message, he realised that the tourer, too, had left the road. He could feel the nauseous lurching as it careered over the uneven ground, and see the trees racing forward to engulf them. . . .

Too late he saw a low branch appear from nowhere. The next moment he took a blow on the side of the head which almost lifted him from the car. He heard Otto give a howl of pain, then the car crashed into a tree and, with a cradle-like rock, came to rest.

NINETEEN

Jake lay sprawled across the seat. Vaguely he knew he'd taken a hit on the head, and in the swirling mists of his mind the swarthy face of Grogan kept appearing. A gentle rhythmic sound penetrated his clearing brain, and realisation came to him that the engine was still running! Instinctively he reached forward to switch it off, and it was then he knew the severity of the blow he'd taken. The sudden movement brought a cold sweat to his forehead, and it was some minutes before the paroxysm passed and his strength began to reassert itself.

Soon he sat up, and it was then he saw that, miraculously, the headlights were still on. Then everything crowded into place—the car, still in one piece; Grogan, gone to perdition, maybe, in the crazed Mercedes; and Otto . . . Otto? Now thoroughly roused, he turned, to see Otto leaning over the wheel, motionless, his face buried in a handkerchief.

"What in hell's name happened, Otto?" he cried. Getting no reply, he reached out and touched him on the shoulder. "Are you all right?"

For a moment the driver made no reply. Then he gave a frantic cry, *"Nein, nein!"* and turned to clutch wildly at Jake, crying, "I'm blind. I'm blind. . . . I cannot see anything."

Horrified, Jake could hardly bear to look. The top half of Otto's face was unrecognisable, but through the mass of blood and torn flesh it was just possible to discern the lacerated eyelids. Trying to be reassuring, he said, "It'll pass presently, Otto, when I've wiped away the blood and cleaned you up. Then, somehow, I've got to get you to a hospital."

The reaction was immediate. "No!" It was almost a scream. "It doesn't matter about me. We've got to get to the schloss . . . we must get to the schloss before morning." He was pulling urgently at Jake's arm again. "Listen. If you could just bathe my eyes, we can go on. I think the car's all right, but you'll have to drive. There's a river on the other side of the road . . ." He stopped, exhausted, then went on, "Get water . . . bathe eyes . . . please. . . ."

Though Jake had heard most of what Otto said, it was his reference to a schloss that caught his attention. So they were making for a castle! He wondered what manner of man he was going to see—a man who lived in a schloss, and who spent a fortune on stamp-collecting : a man feared by his employees presumably, and a man who carried anonymity to absurd lengths.

"O.K., Otto," he cried breezily. "I'll try." He felt under the dash. "Great stuff," he said. "I've found a torch. That'll help."

He went round to Otto's side to switch off the lights. He was on the point of leaving when the thought came to him that he should, perhaps, warn him about Grogan : warn him that Grogan might be on the prowl. Yet, from the speed the Merc charged into the trees and disappeared, this hardly seemed possible. He glanced down at Otto, still leaning forward, the bloodstained handkerchief over his face. Poor devil! He'd be no match for anyone in his present state.

"That driver," he said, "the driver of the Mercedes. . . . I ought to tell you he's dangerous; he's been trying to get me ever since I set out to meet you. Been following me all the way from Ostend."

"He'll be dead," muttered Otto, disinterestedly. "Didn't you see the speed the car went into the trees?"

"But supposing he's not? You'd never see him if he came."

"He's dead . . . and I've got a gun." He reached forward, and almost immediately Jake felt something pushed towards him. "Here—take this, just in case."

Jake switched on the torch, and saw that Otto had handed him a flick-knife—a murderous-looking weapon. There seemed no point in mentioning he'd already got a gun in his pocket.

Using the torch sparingly, he picked his way across the clearing and quickly found the road. Tiptoeing across, he stood for a while in the darkness, listening. Strange how, even on the quietest of nights, the stillness of the pine woods is never complete. Could he hear strange rustlings? Some small creature, maybe, or was it, perhaps, some human prowler? His imagination was playing tricks: he gave a nervous laugh. Flicking on the torch, he could see where the Mercedes had left the road and ploughed through the undergrowth. Treading carefully, he moved forward, but after a few steps he stopped short, realising he was at the edge of a slope where the land fell steeply away. The thin beam of light revealed few trees and little undergrowth immediately below him: it was obvious Grogan's car had plunged down this escarpment. Otto's words, "He'll be dead," came to mind; it seemed Otto must be right!

As, slipping and sliding, Jake began his descent, his torch began to flicker—the battery was giving out! From now on he would have to feel his way, using the torch only when absolutely necessary. At last the ground levelled out, and he knew he had reached the bottom. Here, peering through the gloom, he caught the vague outline of a familiar shape just ahead of him. Now he must use the torch. Yes! It was the Mercedes. By the flickering beam he saw the big car lying upside down, with one door wrenched from its hinges, a battered and twisted wreck. No one could have been in such a crash and lived. Using the torch, he climbed on to the wreckage and peered in through the door space. He drew back hastily, dousing the light—Grogan was not there!

A momentary fear clutched at his throat—the man must be somewhere: perhaps close at hand, waiting to spring. Jake stepped hurriedly from the car and, slipping noiselessly away, crouched in the darkness expectantly. Listening intently, a sound came to his ears. It was not the snap or crackle of a twig, but the chatter of running water. Here, so close that it was a wonder he'd not fallen into it, was the river he'd been looking for. He risked the torch again and breathed a sigh of relief. Grogan would give him no further trouble, for the Mercedes had come to rest hard by the river's edge. Now he could see it all: see the car plunging headlong down the slope, see it leap and turn over, see the wrenched-off door fly into the air, and the luckless Grogan flung into the deep, fast-flowing water. Was this truth or fantasy? Whatever had happened, he'd been away from Otto long enough—he must get back without further delay.

It was as he knelt to get some water from the river that he spotted something trapped in an eddy. Retrieving it, he knew then that his surmise was no fantasy: it was a hat—black and limp. On the inside, by the beam of the dying torch, he saw two metal letters—'D.G.'. Now, for the first time since he'd crossed from Dover, he felt really secure. At last he knew again the feeling of freedom. Hudson, Poxy, Chesney, and now Grogan! No longer was there need for caution. Smiling, he turned his back on the river and began to retrace his footsteps.

Difficult as it was, he made steady progress and was soon at the top. He leant against a tree for a moment to get back his wind. Here, at the side of the road, the darkness was intense, and it soon came to him that he hadn't the least idea where to look for the tourer. The torch was useless now. He raised his voice, calling to Otto to switch on the lights, but there was no reply. He called again—louder: it was impossible that he should have strayed out of earshot.

Again silence! Again no lights!

A feeling of unease crept over him. He shouldn't have left Otto for so long. He knew he dared not leave the road now and wander off into the woods in the dark. Perhaps if he waited a car would come along—then there'd be some light. He stood for several minutes, hoping—then in the far distance came the whisper of an approaching car. There was ample time to move off the road and take cover behind a tree before the headlights swung into view. In the advancing beam of light Jake saw the clearing almost opposite him, and a vague shadow he knew to be Otto's car.

He was across the road and heading for the tourer before the lights had disappeared. He called again for Otto to put on the lights, but he still got no response. It mattered little now, for almost at once his outstretched hand came in contact with the cold metal of the car.

"All is well, Otto," he cried. "I've got water . . . soon have you right." He moved round to the driver's side of the car and could see the faint outline of Otto's head resting across the steering-wheel—just as he'd left him. The man must be really ill. "Otto!" he cried. "Speak to me."

He heard an answering groan, curiously muffled, and as the shadow before him moved he caught the odour of stale cigar. *Then Grogan's head came up, and stubby fingers gripped him round the throat!*

It was the surprise of the attack that made it so one-sided; and Grogan knew this. He determined to keep the car door between them as a shield; this he guessed might prevent Jake using his hands. But Jake, recovering quickly from the immediate shock, had already sensed this, and when he felt his head being forced down on to the top of the door, he braced his hands and knees against the car and gave a savage heave. Merciful heavens! It was a wonder he hadn't decapitated himself. Coloured lights flashed before his eyeballs, and blinding pain shot across his shoulder. Yet the effort paid off, for the imperfectly shut door burst open and he staggered back, bringing Grogan with him.

As they rolled over on the ground Jake struggled desperately to free himself, but though he regained his feet Grogan's fingers were biting deep, and no matter what he attempted the death-hold remained. A feeling of desperation came over him: he had to have air, he was getting light-headed. He took a grip on himself, and got his fist and forearm between the encircling hands and forced them apart. The sweat rolled from his forehead, but as the grip slackened his greedy lungs drew in the life-giving air.

The respite was but momentary, for now the iron fingers had closed again round his throat. Maddened now, he tried everything—kicking and pummelling—but all to no avail; every part of the man, it seemed, was made of steel. Now Jake's struggles were weakening again, his blows losing their power. His mind began to race. Events, things and people danced before his eyes. Among them, clear-cut, he saw a grim-faced Nella—gun in hand—covering a gaping Hudson. His racing mind froze! *The gun! The .22!* What in hell was wrong with him that he hadn't thought of it before?

His fingers closed over the butt, and the gun was out of his pocket. Maybe Grogan felt the movement, or maybe it was just instinct, but as the gun came out the man gave a vicious lunge, almost bringing them both to the ground, and Jake felt the .22 slip from his grasp. Now he knew the end must be near. Swaying back and forth in the darkness, he knew his strength was almost spent: he seemed powerless to free himself from those pitiless fingers. His lungs were bursting—his eardrums booming. His mind wandered: it was Hudson now who had him by the throat, squeezing his life away. Even so, his face twisted into a maniac smile, for he remembered that at any moment the 'pencil' would do its magic work! Then, balancing on the very edge of consciousness, he knew it was not Hudson: there was no 'pencil'. Then something in his brain, some hidden reserve, called him back—"The knife . . . the knife!" it screamed.

The mist cleared. Otto's flick-knife!

Praise God—it was still in his pocket. In a moment it was out. This time he made no mistake. Gripping it fiercely, he got an arm behind Grogan and, calling on his last reserves, plunged the knife between the shoulder-blades. He felt the massive body shudder and sink under him. As if trying to say something, the dying man gave a hoarse croak and slid to the ground. Then Jake was on his face among the pine cones, drawing in great gasps of air.

TWENTY

"ONE more village—*Ragensdorf*—then it's only a kilo-metre." Otto's voice was hardly audible against the sound of the engine.

Almost at once, in the pale first light of dawn, the sign "*Ragensdorf*" came into view and they were climbing the last hill.

"You were right," Jake replied. "I didn't think it would be possible—you must know every metre of the road."

Otto gave a non-committal grunt: it was obvious he was in great pain. The accident had been more than enough— to say nothing of what he'd had to take from Grogan!

It was when Otto was waiting in the car for Jake's return that Grogan had crept up on him and knocked him out. After that, he'd bundled him into the boot and climbed into the driving-seat, ready for his successful impersonation. Jake had no idea how long Otto had remained unconscious, but it was while he was getting back his wind that he first heard the tapping coming from the direction of the car. Wondering if this could possibly be Grogan, he had forced himself to his feet, staggered across to the car and switched on the sidelights. He turned, and at once saw Grogan some two or three yards away, lying on his back in a pool of blood.

As Jake gazed down at the face of the dead man a sense of guilt passed over him. He'd killed a man! This was perhaps murder! He froze at the thought. Supposing a passer-by saw the car lights and stopped. . . .

Who would believe his story?

Who would believe it was self-defence?

There was not even Otto as witness! Otto! Where was he? What had happened? This was no time to panic—first thing was to move the body away. Calmer now, he turned Grogan over, and with fingers that shook withdrew the knife. Then he dragged him away into the darkness.

It was when he got back to the car that the tapping began again. Then he heard a moan, and realised that it was coming from the boot. Poor Otto! He was alive, but in a bad state, though fairly alert mentally. As Jake cleaned up his eyes he told him everything that had happened.

"We must get away at once," said Otto, "before anyone sees us here. We must not be involved. We will throw the knife over the bridge at the bottom of the hill."

When he'd got Otto in tolerable shape, Jake stressed once again that he should be taken to a hospital straight away. It was vital his eyes should have proper medical attention as soon as possible. "If I stop the next car that comes along we'd have you in hospital in no time . . ."

"No, no," broke in Otto excitedly. "If we did that every policeman in the area would be on to us before the day was out. They'd find the car, then the body. No: we must not get involved. My eyes are of no importance compared to . . ." He stopped suddenly, then, calming himself, went on, "We're not going to any hospital, we're going to the schloss. There's a dead body in the bushes and this affects you equally. We must go now. Our car will be all right, I'm sure—but it is you who must drive."

Jake knew Otto was speaking the truth. The last thing he wanted was involvement in Grogan's killing.

The car had suffered only negligible damage, and Jake was soon edging it out into the road again. Otto kept impressing on him that, whatever happened, they must not be seen. "It would be a disaster if a passing motorist saw us and got our number or even a description of us," he warned. The job was soon done, and after a few minutes

Jake was quite at home at the wheel. It seemed almost impossible that Otto could give him such precise details of the route they were to take. His eyes were bandaged now, yet so exact were his directions that rarely, if ever, was a wrong turning taken.

Through the remainder of the night they motored steadily—passing through a score of villages. Presently the blackness around them grew less and soon the greying sky was shot with streaks of gold as the dawn came bustling over the horizon. They passed the village of Ragensdorf, and then they were breasting the last rise. Otto's voice came to him. "Careful!" he warned. "It's a hairpin bend at the top."

Jake eased off, and they rounded the corner. "We've done it," sighed Otto. "If you stop here you'll see the *Schloss Ragensee*—on the island." Jake jammed on the brakes and, leaping from the car, crossed to a stone wall and looked down.

Before him the land fell away steeply, and a thousand feet below—a sheet of blue—lay the mile-wide expanse of water he was to know as the *Ragensee*. In the centre of the lake was a tiny island, and on the island the schloss : grey-walled yet picturesque, its solitary pointed turret casting a long shadow across the tranquil water. On the mainland, reaching out into the lake, was a narrow jetty, and nearby a cluster of dwellings crowded by the water's edge.

As he stood gazing at the panorama he wondered what manner of man lived here, isolating himself on this lonely island. What could he be—misanthrope, devout collector, or fugitive? A fugitive? He shivered, and a sudden feeling of unease passed over him.

A tortuous downhill drive brought them to the jetty. Here the narrow road passed between the cluster of houses to form its one and only village street.

Stopping the car as directed, Jake said, "Here we are, by the jetty."

"Good. Tell me . . . are there any craft tied up?"

"Yes, there's one . . . a dinghy of sorts, with an outboard motor."

"That'll be it." Otto sounded weaker than ever. "Leave the car here," he went on, "and help me get on board."

It was only after he'd settled Otto and was listening to his directions as to how to start the engine that Jake remembered Nella's cigarette-case and compact. He felt in his pocket—they were still there. He remembered her near-hysteria as she implored him to do as she said, and he wondered what excuse he could make to leave Otto. Then he said, "I've left my pipe in the car . . . must get . . .only be a minute."

"Oh . . . all right," grudgingly. "But hurry, I feel terrible."

As Jake retraced his steps along the wooden jetty he remembered passing a sort of general store a few yards back. Leaving the jetty, he quickly reached the shop. He glanced up and down the street—not a soul in sight : hardly surprising—it was not yet 5 o'clock ! Feeling in his pocket, he pulled out the powder-compact and laid it on the ground by the shop window. As he walked away, wondering what to do with the cigarette-case, he noticed a man strolling towards him. He could only just have appeared on the scene : Jake doubted if he'd seen him put down the compact. He was a stocky man, dressed in a check shirt and a pair of dark green leather shorts. A 'local', obviously : the problem of the cigarette-case was solved! As he approached, the man muttered a grudging "*Morgen*".

Jake stopped, put a finger to his lips and pointed to the dinghy. "Do you speak English?" he asked in an under-tone. The man shrugged his shoulders, and gave him a vacant look. Then, from the dinghy, came an urgent call. "Hurry, please. . . . I feel dreadful." There was no time to explain. Acting on impulse, Jake took the cigarette-case from his pocket and thrust it into a claw-like hand. Then he turned and raced for the jetty. As they moved off he cast a look shorewards. Already the cigarette-case was open and its contents were being examined. Jake smiled as he turned and steered the boat out into the lake.

A few minutes later, in one of the lakeside cottages, a heavy-bosomed *Frau* twisted the cigarette-case in her work-grimed hands. "Have nothing to do with it, Helmut," she cautioned. "They are strange folk at the schloss . . . not like it was when the monks were there. Keep the money, and throw the rest in the lake."

TWENTY-ONE

JAKE settled himself in the dinghy and headed for the island. As the distance lessened it was possible to see things in more detail. The schloss covered the greater part of the island, and on one side came right down to the water's edge. On the other it was bounded by a patch of scrub through which ran a narrow walk leading to a primitive landing-stage. The far end of the walk led to a paved fore-court in front of the massive iron-gated entrance to the castle. The gates were bounded on either side by a high stone wall completely surrounding the schloss, which rose, grim and forbidding, to a height of four storeys. Viewed close at hand, its only redeeming feature was the tall, pointed tower at one corner.

Steering the boat in the direction of the landing-stage, Jake saw two men issue from a small postern gate in the wall and come racing towards him. They were gesticulating and making extraordinary noises. He throttled back the Seagull engine, and the dinghy slid in over the polished surface of the water and came to rest by the rotting timbers of the jetty. The men reached out and, grasping the gun-wale, made the boat fast. The difficult journey from Ostend was ended. Jake had arrived!

Concerned for Otto, he called to the men for help to get him ashore quickly. It was only then, as he watched them gesticulating to each other, that he realised there was some-thing unusual, grotesque even, about them. They were twins for a certainty, and were tall and heavily built. They had heavy-jowled, unhealthy-coloured faces, and large, close-cropped heads, but the oddest thing about this curious pair was their voices. As they busied themselves getting Otto ashore, they jabbered incessantly: expressive noises, yet to Jake incomprehensible.

"You'd do well to get Otto indoors and to bed at once," he advised. "He's had a bad time."

One of the twins turned towards him, frowning. "Halla hol ajowah," he replied, waving his arms furiously.

Jake was baffled. He'd forgotten the language problem —but this was no language at all! He watched the other man move away from the landing-stage with Otto in his arms, and, hearing him mutter a string of unintelligible sounds, suddenly grasped the truth. They were deaf mutes! The man at his side pushed him forward roughly. "Wollo, wollo," he cried, finger pointed, face glowering. Jake's temper flared, but the protest died on his lips. What use were words? He turned angrily, and began walking towards the castle.

They soon reached the forecourt, and as they approached the main entrance a bearded face peered furtively from behind the wall. An instant later a small man came out and opened the gates—just enough for them to pass through singly. Jake followed the leader through, and found himself in a large quadrangle. Then the gates crashed to, and he heard the grate of the key in the lock. Involuntarily he gave a shiver: the place had the air of a prison. Without thinking, his hand moved towards his trousers pocket, and he felt the reassuring bulge of Nella's .22, which he'd recovered from near Grogan's body.

It was while crossing the quadrangle that he noticed the floodlights at each corner. Curious, he thought, that the owner should imagine a building of such meagre architectural appeal worth illuminating, especially as, seemingly, visitors were not encouraged. As they mounted some stone steps leading to a handsome, much weathered oak door, he he heard the man behind him trip, and felt him stumble into him. The big fellow would have fallen heavily had he not clutched at Jake to save himself. Recovering his balance, this strange man, his face impassive, made no queer noises of protest or thanks, but, aiming a savage kick at the steps, turned to point a finger towards the door which had now been opened from within. As Jake was about to enter he noticed above the door—carved in the stone—the words *Deus vobiscum*. A thought flashed through his mind—was the *Schloss Ragensee* a monastery, perhaps?

Passing from the brilliance of the early morning sunlight into the gloom of the interior, he could at first see little. Then, his eyes adjusting themselves, he saw they were in a lofty panelled chamber, whose stone-flagged floor led across to a wide, imposing staircase. Apart from a large refectory table, with a few chairs round it, the room was without furniture. They turned into a corridor, also magnificently panelled, and as Jake followed the man in front he was seized from behind and given a vicious push, which sent him careering down the passage. This was too much! Furious, he whipped round to give the lout the lesson of his life, when close at hand he heard a calming voice. "Come in, Mr Standish. You have been delayed, I fear."

His anger sidetracked, he turned again to see he was by an open door leading to a small, book-lined room. Behind a modern desk—his face smiling—sat a man, perhaps in his early forties. His well-groomed fair hair, thinning at the temples, was brushed straight back from his pale face. His clothes were immaculate, but the most striking feature about the man was his eyes. These, pale, ice-cold and penetrating, gave an immediate clue to his character. Jake disliked him instantly.

The man spoke again, in precise English. "I fear my menials, in their anxiety to serve me well, are apt to be a trifle truculent. You must forgive them."

Somewhat mollified, Jake contrived a smile. "Well," he answered, "I must admit I find their methods a bit . . . barbaric."

"You should bear with them. They are quick-tempered,

I know, but Stefan here, and his brother Ivan, are deaf and dumb."

"I'd gathered that. Nevertheless, I wonder you can tolerate them."

"They have their uses." Though the reply was curt, the next words had an ingratiating ring to them. "I feared you'd had an accident on the journey—some little difficulty?"

"It's been nothing but difficulties since I set out to get here."

"For which you have been well paid." This with a sneer.

Jake took the point. "We won't go into that," he answered shortly. "I'm more concerned now to know what's being done for your man, Otto. He's in a bad way."

"Have no fear, Otto will be all right. Ivan will see to him."

"Ivan!" Jake groaned. "Don't you realise the fellow needs medical attention. He could lose his sight."

"There are other, more important, matters to discuss."

It was then, as Jake looked again into those cold eyes, that a feeling passed over him that the face was familiar. Somewhere, he was certain, he'd seen it before—but whether in the flesh or in a photograph he had no idea. His thoughts were interrupted.

"Mr Standish! I'm talking to you. I asked you a question." The voice was querulous, bringing out the worst in Jake.

"Then repeat it."

The eyes opposite him flashed. "I want the packet," he spat. "Please hand it over without delay." A look of suspicious crossed the features. "You have it, of course?"

Jake took a look over his shoulder. "Do we need him?" he enquired, pointing at Stefan posted by the door.

The man gave a forced laugh. "A whim of mine. Talk freely; he cannot hear." As he spoke the door opened, and Jake saw Ivan enter and stand beside his brother. It seemed his earlier fears were well-founded : he was a prisoner! "I understand," he drawled. "Bodyguards!"

A ghost of a smile crossed the austere features. "As I have already said, they have their uses. Come now—the packet."

But Jake was in no mood to hurry. He looked across at the man at the desk. This was no philatelist : no genuine collector! He struggled to remember where he'd seen him : who he was. What reason could the man have for treating him in this way? He was glad now he'd picked up Nella's gun after the fight. If it came to a showdown . . . Instinctively his hand moved for reassurance towards his pocket, but as his fingers groped in the emptiness he found there the chagrin showed on his face.

"Ha!" The cry had a note of triumph. "So Stefan has done his work well. A good picker of pockets—if a trifle dim-witted."

So it was Stefan! He might have known. Must have whipped the gun as he stumbled on the steps. Neat—but to fall so easily to such an old gag!

"I'm waiting, Standish."

"You have the advantage over me, Mr . . .?" answered Jake pointedly. "Suppose you tell me your name."

There was a silence while the man pondered. "Well, why not?" he answered at last. "They call me Ixion here. But not because I murdered my father-in-law." He gave a humourless laugh. "You know your Greek mythology, of course?"

The tone of condescension stung Jake. "What in hell is all this about?" he blazed. "I demand . . ."

"*Shut up!*" Ixion spat the words. "Understand this," he thundered. "No one here demands things, except me." Eyes flashing, he gave a signal to the men at the door. They closed on Jake immediately, and before he could resist had seized him on either side in a grip from which escape seemed impossible.

"Now," said Ixion, coming from behind the desk. "Where is it?"

There was no point in procrastinating. "Attached to a chain around my neck."

Slim fingers fumbled beneath his collar, then the chain was grasped and jerked roughly away. Interested to see what it was he'd carried across Europe—Nella had sworn it was a stamp—Jake kept his eyes on Ixion. Now the thing was delivered, he thought, he'd soon be a free man. Free to get back to Nella. Free to . . . He stopped dreaming. Ixion was unpacking the parcel—his back to them. For a few seconds the room was in silence. Then unexpectedly Ixion's hand thundered to the desk. He whipped round. "What trick is this?" he roared, his face ghastly, his mouth twitching.

"I don't understand . . ."

"Don't lie to me. The packet's empty!"

"It can't be." The surprise was genuine.

"It's empty, I tell you." The eyes were smaller: the voice more menacing. "Talk, Standish. If you value your life."

Jake was dumbfounded. What had gone wrong? Could Nicco have mixed the packets? Impossible! Then suddenly the unexplained incident at Liege came back to him: the drugging! Only then did the ugly truth hit him, sending his hopes, his dreams, crashing. *So she had lied.* "Nella!" Her name slipped from his lips.

Ixion was on it in a flash. "What was that?" he demanded. "You said something . . . a person's name, maybe? Out with it."

Sick at heart, and wondering why she'd deceived him, Jake thought fast. "It was nothing," he shot back. "You're mistaken. There has been no trickery. I undertook to bring the packet to you, and I've done just that. If you've any complaints—make 'em to Gostoli. So now, if you'll call off your bodyguards, I'll be on my way."

Ixion gave a laugh. It was not a pleasant sound. "*Very* funny," he scoffed. His eyes fixed Jake in a gaze that seemed to penetrate to the very brain. "Bluff won't help, you know," he continued. "We play for high stakes at the *Schloss Ragensee*—very high stakes. You don't fool me,

Standish. You know something, and I'm going to find out what it is. Our methods are very effective. . . ."

The telephone on the desk rang shrilly. Curious he'd not noticed it, thought Jake : maybe his chance would come. He could phone Nella, perhaps. Nella? What good would that do? Was she not playing some deep game of her own? And he no more than a pawn in it. All along she must have known he was walking into this—yet she hadn't . . .

Across his bitter thoughts came Ixion's voice, strained and petulant, shouting into the telephone. "I'm busy, damn you. Otto must wait."

Jake caught the tinny sound from the other end. Then Ixion burst out angrily, "The packet's empty . . . empty, I tell you. We've been fooled. Don't you understand?"

The voice at the other end persisted, and the anger in Ixion's voice faded. "Otto thinks it important, eh?" he muttered. "Something about a woman? I see!" A crafty look crossed his features, and his eyes rested on Jake. Then, thinking aloud, he drawled, "Ye-es, they do work in pairs —often." He listened again, then rapped briskly, "She'll have to be brought in, that's all. But I'll come up and talk to him myself." He banged the receiver down, got up and crossed the room. At the door he paused and forced a sickly grin. "Pity Otto's feeling better, isn't it? Says you've got a dame tucked away." He gave a laugh. *"Cherchez la femme*, eh? Ah well, you'll be glad to talk presently." He raised a hand to Stefan, pointing to the far side of the room, and was gone.

The two men, working to a familiar routine doubtless, knew what was required. Leaving Jake in the custody of his brother, Stefan moved across to the wall opposite, selected one of the books, and gave it a hard push. Instantly an entire section swung outward to reveal a dark cavity. It needed little imagination to guess their intentions, and Jake knew the time for action had come. This was the moment : with Stefan by the cavity maybe there'd be time to deal with Ivan! He gave a sudden wrench to tear his arm free, and with the accuracy which comes only from expert training kicked Ivan's legs from under him. He didn't wait to see him fall, but, whipping round, sent a fist crashing into Stefan's jaw. It was a glancing blow, but hard enough to send him swaying backward. There was not a moment to lose. Jake raced for the door; but he had reckoned without his host—*it was locked on the outside!* Then Nella's gun crackled, and he heard the spatter of bullets in the woodwork above his head. Stefan, recovering miraculously, had gone trigger-happy. There was only one thing to do. Jake raised his arms.

Mortified by the failure of his escape bid, he watched dully as Ivan collected a torch and led the way into the cavity and down some stone steps. He followed passively enough, but when he reached the top step Stefan, who was following, hit him hard between the shoulder-blades. There were six steps, and missing all of them Jake landed heavily on the uneven stone floor, where he lay dazed and shaken. He heard Stefan, grunting in satisfaction, clump down towards him. Then he was given a kick, and felt the cold muzzle of the gun against his neck. Sheer will-power brought him to his feet, and he lurched down the dark passage, guided by the light of Ivan's torch ahead.

It was a nightmare journey. Bruised and giddy from the fall, he saw little. Presently he became aware that he was climbing an iron staircase. The exertion made his head swim. But at last he was on a small landing, and Ivan was opening a door. Then Stefan pushed him from behind, and he staggered forward. In a daze, he heard the door slam and the key turn : and he was alone. For a few minutes he stood swaying while his eyes grew accustomed to the light coming from an embrasure in the wall at one end of the passage-like room. He could see ahead a dirty mattress on the floor. He stumbled towards it, and slumped down gratefully.

It was late afternoon when he awakened. He stretched warily and gave a grunt of satisfaction, for, apart from a

F

heavy head and some body bruises, he was unharmed. As he lay there he became aware of a raging thirst, though strangely he was not hungry. His mind went back to his last meal, and he remembered how Nella had merely toyed with the dinner. He remembered her strange behaviour throughout the evening, and again he sensed the conviction that she'd known what had lain ahead for him. Equally, he knew now that he loved her, would forgive her anything, and give anything to be with her again. He believed, too, that he knew her true feelings about him; her expression in an unguarded moment had so often betrayed her. Yet, why should she allow him—encourage him, even—to walk headlong into danger? And there was danger. One had only to take a look at those ice-cold, penetrating eyes!

Thoughts of Ixion brought a cloud to his face. What was it he'd said? "She'll have to be brought in, that's all." That could only mean he'd send for her: get her to the castle by some trick. He shuddered at the thought of Nella at the mercy of the man. Maybe she'd have left the hotel—but why, where would she have gone? Then he remembered how she'd clung to him: said it was imperative she knew where he was going. Did she intend to follow? He sighed. It was all too damned involved. . . .

He got up and took stock of his surroundings. The room, in appearance a boarded-up passage, was some fifteen feet long but only six feet wide. There was one stone wall, the other three sides being constructed of wood. In the stone wall was set an embrasure—a rectangular aperture almost two feet in depth. It was wide enough to get his shoulders through. He wriggled into it, and craned his neck. . . .

His hands clawed at the stonework for support as he looked down at the breathtaking view. Below him—a dizzy distance below—was the lake. Across the water, shimmering in the warm sunshine, he glimpsed the lakeside village, and beyond, dominant and majestic, the snow-capped peaks. It was a spectacle to delight any artist, but for Jake it held no thrill, for it showed him his whereabouts. He was in the tower at the corner of the castle—a hundred feet or more above the lake. The bitter truth came to him : *from here there could be no escape.*

Dragging himself from the embrasure, he crossed to the table and slumped into a rickety chair to contemplate the bleakness of his discovery. But as he sat there he became increasingly aware that there was yet another bitter truth to be faced. His thirst! What had at first been a raging thirst was now fast becoming a scourge to plague him more with each passing minute. Perhaps this was how they intended to deal with him. Was there no way he could convince them that he had nothing to tell; no secret to disclose?

Later, his throat a desert, it was only by strength of will that he could keep in check a feeling of panic. He returned to the embrasure to call loudly, wildly even, to a dead world. Sometimes he beat his fists against the door set in the wooden partition, but no one came. A feeling of despair came over him as slowly, almost unnoticed, twilight filled the room. Then came the dark. But at last he heard it. . . . Someone was mounting the stairs. As in a dream he saw Stefan in the doorway, hurricane-lamp in one hand, gun in the other. Behind him, bearing a tray, came Ivan. . . .

Jake seized a brimming Stein in two hands. . . .

Almost half the night was gone, and Jake was sleeping. Now that his wild thirst had been assuaged his sleep was deep. Yet suddenly, an hour before the dawn, he jumped awake. He listened intently, his senses instantly alert. All was quiet, yet intuition—or was it telepathy?—told him something was afoot. In a flash he was in the embrasure, gazing out upon a darkened world. Then the moon burst forth to shed light upon the surroundings. Nothing had changed : all was as still as when he'd last looked out. But was it? Could it be that he had imagined a slight movement in the water a mere stone's throw from the jetty? Frowning, he glanced up at the cloud which had just masked the moon. But it was only a momentary obstruction. Then he saw what had attracted his attention—a small rowing-boat was drifting slowly towards the shore. As he watched, he caught the faint outline—ghostly almost—of a crouching figure in the stern. A moment later the craft was lost within the shadow of the landing-stage.

Jake waited—excited and impatient—conscious of a strange yet powerful feeling of involvement. The seconds slipped by, and nothing happened. But now the moon was dimmed, and by a cloud mass so vast he knew he would see no more. He waited, staring into the darkness, tense and unaccountably full of foreboding. To his straining ears the silence was almost unbearable. Why should he feel like this? Why this feeling of belonging?

Then, shattering in its nearness, came the sound of a shot, followed by running footsteps and the shouting of men. Straining forward in the embrasure, there came into view the shadowy forms of a mêlée below him, but even as he looked the scuffling and shouting died down. He heard the murmur of voices and the footfall of men grow fainter, until all was silent again. Suddenly, ringing clear and defiant in the still air, he heard the cry of a woman's voice. "Keep your filthy hands off me, you scum."

Jake fell back into the room, shaking, his face blanched. Yet, subconsciously, his mind had never been in doubt.

TWENTY-TWO

PATIENCE was almost at breaking-point. The man was almost beside himself. "Now, young woman." The voice was still controlled. "We'll try again."

Reaching in the pocket of her slacks for a cigarette, Nella looked across at Ixion, unflinching. "I shouldn't bother," she yawned. "I have no intention of saying anything."

"Blast you! You *will* talk." The voice rose to a shriek as the words spat from his thin lips. He jerked the telephone towards him, and a moment later he barked just two words into the mouthpiece. "Come . . . now."

On the far side of the room, tied hand and foot, sat Jake, grim-faced and apprehensive. On either side of him were the deaf and dumb twins—their great bodies noxious in their nearness.

Now, as Ixion waited, a silence loaded with grim anticipation and foreboding descended on the room. Jake recalled those hours of waiting, when the dawn came in and the sun rose higher and higher. He had begun to wonder if news of Nella would ever reach him. But at last, several hours after daybreak, they had come for him. As he climbed the steps where he'd fallen so heavily the previous night, he tried to convince himself it would not be she. But, deep down, he knew there was no mistaking the voice which had rung out with such clarity in the small hours. Stepping through the aperture and into the room, and seeing her lounging in a chair opposite Ixion—serene and quite lovely—her name escaped from his lips.

"Nella!"

She gave only the merest inclination of her head. "Hallo, Jake," she returned gravely.

So impersonal had seemed the greeting that for a moment he wondered if she and the man at the other side of the table were partners in some obscure plot. But as the thought came to him he was given proof to the contrary, for, twisting in his chair, Ixion turned towards him. "Standish," he said, "I trust you will not deny that this young woman is a friend of yours." He waited, as if expecting a reply, then continued, "The lady prefers to be awkward, and refuses to answer my questions. Don't you think that is rather unwise?"

"How should I know? That depends upon what you've asked her."

Ixion banged his fist on the desk. "*Here* she does as I say," he thundered. "I'm warning you both. . . ."

As the man ranted, some sudden expression brought it all back. He knew now where he'd seen the face, the cold penetrating eyes, the ruthless mouth. Four or five years ago it was—in the newspapers: the photographs, the publicity. Now he knew, beyond doubt, who the mysterious Ixion was. He remembered the outcry from Press and public alike when it became known that Felix Ionides—a British citizen of Greek origin—Senior Administrator in a top secret branch of the Atomic Energy Commission, had defected to Russia! It was bad enough when they learned he was missing, but when news of the defection burst the clamour was deafening. Why, of all people, had a foreigner been appointed? True, he was, among other things, a brilliant scientist, but why? Why? Would we never learn?

The discovery came as a shock to Jake, for now the affair began to assume dangerous proportions: there was more to this than dodging the Customs! It could well be that he— and perhaps Nella—had unwittingly got involved in something as formidable as international politics.

"Listen!" Ixion was shouting. "Get your lady friend to

tell me why she came here, who she is working for, and what she has done with the packet."

"You ask her."

Ixion swallowed hard. "We intend to have this information," he said. "If you've any regard for this . . . lady, you'd better tell her to start talking. We have methods, you know." His eyes dilated. We could, for instance, get interested in her finger-nails. . . ."

Jake shuddered. He saw a sudden look of fear come into Nella's eyes. "You'd never dare," he choked. "Even the traitorous Felix Ionides would hardly sink that low."

Ixion's expression hardly charged. His *sang-froid* was remarkable. For a moment he was silent, then, "I see," he said at last. He paused, and went on cryptically, "I'm almost beginning to feel sorry for you, Standish." He turned towards Nella, his voice threatening. "We'll soon have you talking, young woman."

Jake knew he meant business. "You'd better talk, Nella," he advised, "if there's anything to tell."

She returned his gaze imperturbably. "He can do as he pleases, Jake," she replied indifferently. "These stupid questions. . . ."

Mastering his fury, Ixion made one more attempt. But it was the complete detachment of the girl that made him seize the telephone and scream the fateful words, "Come . . . now!"

For nearly a minute the room was in silence. But then the door opened and a tall, grey-haired man entered and strode briskly past Jake.

"Why didn't you bring them?" asked Ixion in a low voice.

"I have them," returned the man equably, throwing a pair of pliers on to the desk.

Ixion seemed jittery. "Grab them, then, and let's get it over with."

A shiver passed over Jake as he watched the man pick up the pliers and move towards Nella. Even now he couldn't believe they'd dare. He glanced towards her, knowing she must have realised; but apart from a disdainful curve of her lips, her face was as composed as when he first entered the room.

Ixion rose to stand over her. "For the last time," he demanded sullenly. "Have you anything to say?"

Jake watched her lips move, and heard the quiet but unfaltering "No." As in a trance, he watched Ixion turn away, muttering thickly, "The obstinate bitch. . . . Give her the treatment."

The tall man grasped Nella's hand. Jake saw the pliers poised. . . .

"Oh no! You can't. . . ." he cried, tugging frenziedly at his bonds. He struggled madly, but the ropes round his hands and feet held fast. Then he was gripped painfully by a twin on either side, and forced into stillness. Blind fury raged in the chaos of his brain, and a red mist swirled behind his eyes. Yet his reason held. Only Nella, he knew, could save herself.

"For God's sake, Nella." It was a cry of desperation.

But it was too late—already the pliers had closed on her thumb-nail. He watched horror-struck, as if in the grip of some macabre nightmare, as the man—his features expressionless—pulled. . . . He saw the blood come oozing from the base and sides of the nail. His head swam again. But a moment later the nausea passed, and he saw both men were standing over the girl.

Ixion's voice was granite. "Now," he was saying, "are you ready to talk, or do you want another dose?"

Nella's hand hung lifelessly at her side, and there was blood dripping to the floor. At the tip of the thumb, terrible to behold, was a great scarlet gash. Her face, white as chalk, wore a fixed expression, as set—but for a faint trembling of the lower lip—as if it were carved in stone.

"*Will* you talk?" screamed Ixion.

It seemed for a moment she was past comprehension. Then, looking up, she said disdainfully, "I will not."

"We'll see about that," cried the tall man. Again the pliers were raised. . . .

"*Stop!*" It was Ixion's voice.

The man turned, still grasping her wrist. Jake could see her bite her lips in agony. "What?" The man was incredulous.

"I said stop," repeated Ixion. "We're wasting our time . . . this won't make her talk."

"What then?"

"Standish." His face shaped into a crafty smile. "I should have thought of it before. We'll give Standish the treatment. Can't you see the girl's in love with him? She'll talk quick enough."

Caught off her guard, Nella's eyes momentarily betrayed her. "See," he cried, pointing. "Was anything more obvious?"

They took Jake in a steely grip and untied his wrists to free one hand. Quickly they lashed his other hand to the back of the chair. He was powerless to move. He saw the tall man step forward—saw the pliers raised—knew the ritual. If Nella could take it, he had no option. . . . He set his teeth : braced himself. . . .

"No!" It was Nella, her voice high-pitched, frantic. "Stop! I'll talk, I'll talk. I'll tell you everything."

Ixion raised a restraining hand. "Talk then," he said.

"I will, I will." It seemed the fight had suddenly gone out of her. Pale, and with eyes averted, she explained that it had been her job to procure the packet. She had managed this simply enough by drugging Mr Standish at Liege. Then she had emptied the packet, resealed it, and returned it to him without his knowledge.

"And where is the . . . thing now?" Ixion's face was twitching.

"Back in England, I trust."

Ixion smothered a curse. "What then?" he flashed. "You'd got the stuff—why didn't you clear out?"

After a pause she spoke. "By then," she said quietly, "I'd

grown to . . . like him. I couldn't bring myself to leave him."

"Yet you allowed him to come on here to no purpose. You must have realised what this would mean."

There was no answer.

Ixion turned towards Jake. "So she made a fool of you," he taunted. "How do you like that?"

Jake said nothing, and Ixion again turned to Nella. "I doubt if there's a word of truth in all this," he said. "Anyway, who is this mysterious employer of yours?"

"I can't possibly divulge that."

"So it's to be the pliers, after all."

Jake saw her sway forward. She seemed on the point of collapse. "Oh, all right," she answered wearily. "His name is . . ."

"Go on."

"His name is . . . Ruberack, and he's an Accountant in London."

"Address?"

"Chancery Gardens . . . that's all I know."

"Very interesting. And I'm supposed to believe all this?"

"It's perfectly true."

"Look at me." He rapped out the words. "How did you find out Standish came here?"

"I supplied him with the means of getting a message to me. He did what was required of him, and a passing tourist did the rest."

"And when you found out, what then? You telephoned your employer?"

"I did not telephone anybody."

His face was demoniac, and he crossed from the desk and seized her hand. Grasping that terrible thumb, he squeezed. "Have you communicated with anyone?" he shouted. "Anyone? Answer me that."

Jake saw the tears spring to her eyes. "Merciful Christ!" He groaned the words.

"Have you?"

"No. I swear it." Her face was desolate, bewildered almost. "I . . . I only followed. It was the only thought in my mind. . . . I had to be with him."

Ixion dropped her hand. "I can verify all this in a few hours, you know. So it had better be true. Not that it'll do you any good—you know too much. Tonight the helicopter comes. By tomorrow you'll both be a long way from here." He pulled his mouth into a sickly grin. "Yes," he muttered, "a long way from here; quite an experience!"

Jake glanced at Nella and their eyes met. Was it imagination, or did he see in hers a strange gleam? Then Ixion gave a perfunctory wave of the hand. "Take them to the bell-tower," he cried, "and God help them if the girl has lied."

TWENTY-THREE

THE only light in the bell-tower came from the louvres set
in the spire high above them. It was a grim prison, entirely
without furniture. He had managed to find some sacks to
spread out as a rude bed for her, and by ripping up a piece
of his shirt had been able to bandage the ghastly wound.
Now, at last, she was sleeping fitfully.

As he sat by her side he wondered how and where it
would all end. The fact that she'd taken the packet from
him meant little compared with her revealing admission.
Even now, with Ixion's threatening words ringing in his
ears, he felt light-hearted : almost carefree. Looking down
at the sleeping girl, he longed to take her in his arms and
tell her. . . . And to think she should feel that way, too!

But presently Ixion's words began to plague him. If they
were to be flown off—to Russia, perhaps—what future was
there for them? What lay ahead—torture, brainwashing,
prison? He shuddered, and at that moment knew that,
come what may, their only hope lay in escape. Though he
had no plan, he knew it would have to be done after dark,
and before the arrival of the helicopter. He sighed. If only
Nicco knew their whereabouts—but neither he nor anybody
else could help. It was entirely up to him. He remembered
Nicco's warning.

Determined to find some means of escape, he began by
searching the chamber. Feeling the walls, he soon discovered that though three were of stone, the fourth was
made of wood. On investigation he found a door leading

into a narrow cupboard, some six feet deep. Moving into it
with arms outstretched, his hands came into contact with
stone : it was the fourth stone wall of the tower. It seemed
that cupboards must have been built along the entire length
of this side. As he was turning, his foot kicked against
something hard. Bending down, he picked up a large chisel.
He smiled : this was better than no weapon at all! As he
was leaving the cupboard he saw something which sent his
hopes soaring : a chink of light was filtering in through a
gap in the boards at his side! Where was this light coming
from? Could it be that here was some secret passage—that
this way lay escape? There was only one way to find out.
Grasping the chisel, he forced it between the boards.
Luckily, he realised in time that this was no ordinary
match-boarding, but good, solid timber. There was only
one way to deal with it : to chip and split it away in small
pieces.

It took half an hour to open up a small gap, but his
excitement rose when he caught a glimpse of a sunlit
passage beyond. Soon he'd enlarged the gap sufficiently to
get a grip on one of the boards. He tore at it fiercely, working it back and forth until at last it came away in his hands.
Now he would know! He thrust his head through the
opening, and gave a groan of disappointment. *Beyond, lit
by the afternoon sun, was the passage-like chamber where
he'd spent the night.* All this time and toil wasted! He
held his head in anguish.

"Jake—Jake! Where are you?" It was Nella, and there
was urgency in her cry.

He was back with her in a flash, and he needed no explanation why she'd called. Heavy footsteps were approaching. He flung on his shirt, and remembered to close the
cupboard door. It was not a moment too soon, for as he
dropped to her side the key grated in the lock and Stefan's
massive bulk filled the doorway. From the light of Stefan's
torch Jake saw a pocket-size man dodge in with a tray of
victuals. He remembered the little man as the custodian of

the castle gates. The man placed the tray on the floor and stood upright, then with mock obeisance said in halting English, "Milord will ring . . . naturally . . . if the fare is not to his liking." His laughter, an infuriating cackle, exploded as he ran to the door. "The bell . . . up in the tower. You could toll it," he chortled.

The door slammed, and they were alone.

More than an hour was to pass before the man's words took on a new meaning. But it was a momentous hour : an hour of truth. At first Nella could not face the food. The pain, she told him, had deadened, but she felt ghastly. By the light from the cupboard door he was able to take his first close look at the horror wrought by the pliers. It was a pitiful sight. The rough bandage—completely saturated —was removed and carefully replaced with another strip of Jake's shirt. It was a long time before he could persuade her to eat. But at last she did so. Presently she looked up at him, and in a weak voice said, "Jake dear, why are you so sweet to me?"

"Nella darling, I . . ."

She interrupted the outburst. "No, Jake! It was silly of me to ask . . . don't say anything . . . out of . . . well, sympathy. I couldn't bear it."

"But, Nella . . ." he began.

"Don't say a thing, Jake," she broke in. "We have things to say to each other—more relevant—but in a whisper, for God's sake. The place may be wired."

He nodded. "You start, then."

"Downstairs," she began softly, "did you, too, believe it all? Am I such a good actress, then?"

His face clouded. "What? Do you mean it was all untrue . . . what you told them, I mean?"

"Sheer fantasy—some of it."

"Why?"

"To gain time, of course. It might help."

"But, Nella! To let them do that to you!" He pointed to her hand. "Why not 'confess' right away?"

"That'd be too obvious. Besides, I didn't intend to tell them a thing. . . ." She stopped suddenly.

"Go on."

"I meant to keep silent. But it was when they started on you. . . ." She laid a hand on his. "Jake dear, I couldn't let them. You'd done no wrong."

"So because of me you told them a pack of lies?"

"Some part of it was lies."

"The part about the drugging—that was true? And about taking the packet?"

She made a wry smile. "Yes. But the man in London— the one I'm supposed to be working for—that was nonsense."

"And the rest of it? All that stuff about . . . being unable to leave me. Nonsense, too, I suppose?" There was bitterness in his voice.

She turned her face away, but her hand was still in his. "I can't blame you for hating me. I did an unforgiveable thing, letting you come here. . . . I could have stopped you. . . ."

"Nella!" The tone of his voice stopped her. "Listen— I don't hate you. But I want you to answer my question. Was it lies—that you couldn't leave me, I mean?"

He waited for a reply, but she was silent. "Well?" he repeated.

Later—an aeon later, it seemed—he felt her hand quicken on his. "Oh, Jake!" It was a cry from the heart. Though barely audible, the two words told him all he needed to know. As his arms went round her she gave a sigh of contentment and pressed herself close to him. Presently she took her lips from his and regarded him gravely. "From all this," she murmured, "I suppose I can take it I'm forgiven?"

"I could forgive you anything, sweetheart—but why, why did you do it?"

For a time she gave no answer. Then he heard her voice, tinged with sadness. "Oh, the uselessness of it all. . . ."

"Why? What?"

"Us! What hope is there?"

He looked down at her, puzzled.

"You really don't know what place this is?"

He shrugged his shoulders. "Some sort of hideout, I suppose. I recognised Ionides as the man who defected."

She made a sudden move to get upright, wincing with pain as her hand touched the floor. "Listen, Jake." Her words came fast. "Certain people in England have known for some time that the Russians had established—not too far from an Iron Curtain country—a secret clearing-house. The sort of place where agents, weapons, formulae, anything, could be assembled for ultimate transmission to Russia. For months its exact location has eluded us. . . ."

His reaction was immediate. "Us?" he broke in.

She went on hurriedly, "Then we found that some completely innocent person had been inveigled into becoming a 'carrier' of . . . something we believed was bound for this secret place. That person was you. My job was to follow you, *and stick to you*, so that you would lead me here. At the same time, I had to prevent, *at any cost*, the . . . thing . . . from reaching any foreign power."

"Yet you insisted it was a stamp."

"I know. But I couldn't tell you the truth then."

"But you can now, eh?"

"It can't make much difference now, I suppose."

"What was it?"

"The prototype of a micro-precision instrument known as the Hoffenmuir Guider Gyro. . . ."

"What the . . ."

"Listen. It's quite revolutionary . . . said to spell death to anti-ballistic missiles. Any foreign power would give its soul for it. The thing took Professor Hoffenmuir five years to perfect."

"And Gostoli, how does he fit in?"

"One of his hired bullies knifed the Professor, and took the prototype. The Professor died."

"I see." Then, after a pause, "So you're what?" He grinned. "A sort of female Bond?"

"Unfortunately, darling, this is a serious business. We're in it up to the neck. You don't imagine Ionides will relent, do you? We know too much . . . know the location of their 'clearing-house'. It'll be Russia . . . or worse . . . for us tonight, unless . . ."

"Unless what?"

She lowered her voice to a mere whisper. "I . . . we, have friends. When the tourist phoned me, and I knew you were at Ragensee, I did make a telephone call."

"But you told Ixion . . ."

"We'd be dead already if he thought I'd lied."

"So you telephoned. Brussels, no doubt?" Tense though the moment was, he couldn't resist it.

She managed to smile. "It was Brussels. We call him 'The Commander'. If anyone can reach us in time, he's the one to do it."

Jake was silent. Then, "But when you phoned him you couldn't have known I was actually at the schloss."

"No. But when he gets to Ragensee he'll realise, like I did, that the castle's the only place."

His mouth straightened. "Then we've got to get out of this accursed tower somehow," he muttered.

"What's beyond the cupboard, where you've been working?"

"No good. I had hopes, but it's just a partitioned-off room. I spent the night in it. Has a secret entrance, and its own stairs. Handy for some foul purpose, I suppose."

"Oh."

"It's got a window of a sort, but what the hell's the good of a window without a rope." He got up and began pacing up and down restlessly. "If only we had a rope," he kept murmuring.

Quite suddenly he brought a fist crashing into the palm of his hand. "The bell," he whispered, his eyes aglow. "The bell! That idiot with the beard . . . what were his exact words? 'The bell up in the tower . . . you could toll it.' In a fever of excitement, he began searching the tower again, muttering, "There must be a rope." A moment later he gave a muffled cry. "Here it is . . . in the corner." In a second she was at his side.

The rope was a foot out from the wall at one corner of the tower. It entered the bell-tower through a hole in the floor, and passed on up into the spire, where it was lost to view. Feverishly, he began to haul it up. It came through the hole easily enough, and as the pile at their side grew, their enthusiasm mounted. "This is terrific," he whispered. "If they used to ring it from the ground floor, we'll get enough."

But as he began again he muttered a curse, for the rope checked in his hand. He pulled hard, and through the hole came the faded 'sally': the rope had come through intact!

Nella smiled. "Is it enough?" she asked anxiously.

"Should have more . . . to be safe." He gazed upwards. Somewhere up there, in the spire, was the bell. Could he sneak a few more feet? Was there a way up?

Presently he found it: a crude wooden ladder nailed to the wall. He put his foot on the first rung. After fifteen feet the ladder petered out. He looked up, and by the shimmer of the louvres could see the vague shape of the bell not far above him. Rejoining Nella, he collected up the chisel. "I think I can get enough," he said, "but it'll take time with this. Keep an ear open, darling, for anyone on the stairs."

It was punishing work, but as the jagged edge of the chisel bit through the last strands, hope surged within him. Now all that remained was to enlarge the opening into the secret room, and wait for the night.

The hours went by, and when darkness came they went through to the embrasure and looked out. Not a light to be seen except the faint flickerings of Ragensee at the other side of the lake. The castle, grey and ghostly against the skyline, was a dead thing: still and silent. Later, Nella slept, but Jake, too keyed-up, kept anxious vigil. Presently, judging it past midnight, they knew the time had come. Everything was in readiness. As they moved again towards the cupboard Nella stopped. "Listen!" she whispered tensely. They stood immovable, hand in hand, scarcely daring to breathe. The minutes passed, then Nella whispered again, "I thought it was outside the door . . . a soft footfall. Must have been mistaken."

They passed through into the secret room. Here Jake tied one end of the rope to a board removed from the partition. Then he wedged the board firmly between the gap he'd made in the cupboard, and secured it with a chair. Testing it, he knew it would hold. He crawled into the embrasure. Outside all was still. He began paying out the rope—down, down, foot by foot. . . .

Back at her side, he said, "Nella, sweetheart, you'll have to go first. Sure you can make it . . . with your hand?"

She gave a sigh that twisted his heart. "Got to," she murmured. Then he was holding her close, caressing her. She slid from his arms, whispered a soft "G'bye," and, grasping the rope, levered herself backwards into the night.

As the silhouette of her head passed from view he crawled into the opening and looked down. It was lighter now, and the agony of fear he was suffering quickly changed to admiration as he watched her steady progress downwards. She had gone some thirty feet: another few seconds and she'd be down. . . .

Then it happened!

Shattering in its suddenness, the castle floodlights came on, and as he gazed helplessly down at Nella—now brilliantly illuminated—he saw a hand below reach out and seize the rope. The next instant she had disappeared from view!

TWENTY-FOUR

He saw at once that Nella had been dragged in through a lower window. They'd found out she'd lied, presumably, so what they'd do to her now wouldn't bear thinking about. With escape so near—to be thus foiled was unbearable. Now that they had found each other, no one was going to take her from him. His brain raced, and he knew surprise was his only chance.

He was facing outwards, in the embrasure. There was no time to turn : every second was precious. Gripping the chisel between his teeth, he seized the rope with both hands and pushed himself out, head first. The sudden jolt to his wrists and arms when his body righted itself was agonising. But his grip held. Then, with feet dangling, he slid down the rope at such speed that he could feel the friction rip the skin from his hands. As he did so, he became aware of the rhythmic 'clack, clack' of the incoming helicopter. Now it was obvious : landing-lights, not flood-lights !

He was there almost before realising it. It was a window, modernish, and sizeable, too. Inside the room a hurricane-lamp was burning. He saw two shadowy figures locked together. . . .

Bracing his feet on the stone sill, he bent his knees and, straightening his legs, hurled himself backwards. He was some five or six feet out from the castle wall before, pendulum-like, he swung back. It was an accurate shot ! Feet first, he was projected in through the window, to land upright in the middle of the room. He heard the sound of the chisel as it fell to the floor. It was Nella he saw first, clinging frenziedly to the tall, grey-haired man. He caught the agony in her face. Even before the man glanced over his shoulder, Jake recognised him. Something in his head snapped, and he could feel the buzzing in his ears.

"Stand back, Nella," he cried, murder in his voice.

The man, tall and menacing, came at him with both fists. But behind Jake's eyes was a mental picture of Nella's blood oozing as the thumb-nail came away. His temples throbbed : at this moment nothing mattered but revenge. With practised ease he sidestepped to avoid those flailing fists. Then, as the fellow stumbled past, Jake caught his wrist with one hand and, with lightning speed, gripped his shoulder. With the skill of an expert he spun the man round, forced the wrist up his back and completed the hold. He knew that at any time the Trussed Arm Lock could be dangerous, but he knew too that, mercilessly applied, bones snapped like twigs.

He heard the elbow go : felt the arm go limp. Uttering a terrified shriek, the grey-haired man slumped to the floor.

It was Nella who heard the other sound. "Footsteps!" she cried. "On the stairs. . . ."

Jake could also hear them now : louder, nearer. "Ixion," he yelled. "Through the window, Quick !"

She hesitated. "And you?"

"I'll follow. . . . Run. . . ."

She raced for the window and, taking the rope in her hands, swung outward. Jake heard a shuffling noise behind him. Then the gun roared. . . . He caught her faint cry and, horrified, saw the twisted expression on her face as she threw her arms in the air. Jesus ! It was certain death from that height. He whipped round. Ixion was in the doorway, a grim smile on his face a smoking revolver in his hand.

"One move, and I'll let loose," he screeched, stepping to one side to allow Stefan to enter. "Grab him," he yelled. Stefan understood.

In Jake's brain something was hammering, beating time to the words "Nella's dead. . . . Nella's dead." He had only one thought : heedless of guns—anything—he flung himself forward. The gun roared again, and he felt a tearing, searing pain in his shoulder; but nothing mattered any more.

Stefan thrust out a great hand to seize him. It was all Jake needed. With a whip-lash action he threw his arm outward, sweeping Stefan's to one side. His other hand came up and, with his fore- and middle-fingers rigid, he struck. It was a terrible blow—but this was life or death. The fingers went home—one in each eye—and Stefan, making an unearthly sound, thrust his hands to his face and staggered to one side. Out of the corner of his eye Jake could see Ixion raising the gun, a Webley Mk. IV, short-barrelled, eminently lethal ! As he ducked it went off with shattering proximity, and he heard the bullet whistle past. Blind rage brought him inspiration. Pivoting a half-circle to bring his back to his adversary, he bent from the waist and got his hands to the floor. The movement was so quick that before Ixion realised the danger he'd delivered a hard backward thrust-kick to his solar plexus. He heard the gun fall to the floor, and as he turned saw Ixion doubled up, face contorted. He was about to go after the gun when, glancing sideways, he saw the grey-haired man—one arm dangling—coming at him. But the blood-lust was in him now. He leapt forward and, seizing the man by the ears, pulled his head forward and down. Then he brought up his knee. . . .

He turned from the appalling sight in time to see Stefan, sightless, feeling his way through the door. But before he could make a move to stop him Stefan had passed from view, and there came an inhuman cry, followed by the sound of a falling body. Stefan had missed the top stair. Jake drew a breath of relief. The fight seemed over.

Maybe it was foolish to look towards the window, foolish to hesitate. But Nella? If he could reach her now perhaps she'd have a chance. The hesitation was but momentary, but for Ixion it was enough! He, too, knew the value of speed. With a tiger-like spring he leapt at the unsuspecting Jake from behind, and got his hands round his throat. There was uncanny strength in those hands, and together they fell to the floor. It was only then, feeling his shoulder stiffen, that Jake realised the extent of the bullet wound, and it was only then the possibility of failure crossed his mind. He had taken a hard knock crashing to the ground, and had fallen face down with Ixion on top, straddling him. No matter what Jake tried, the murderous grip held, sapping his strength. His mind went back to the Grogan fight : that fight to the death. But now there was no knife to help him. Powerless to move in this iron grip, he felt his head raised, then banged to the floor. It was sheer agony. More than once his head was brought up to repeat the process, and each time he grew weaker. Through his deadened senses he could hear the helicopter overhead preparing to land. What little hope he had must now be gone! Yet it was Ixion who made the mistake. He caught sight of the Webley—only a few feet distant.

Grabbing for the gun, he released one hand and shifted his arm so that Jake's neck was firmly gripped in the crook of his elbow. Jake could see Ixion's free hand stretching out, and his fingers clawing the boards to gain the extra inches needed to reach the gun. It was at that moment, to one side of him, he saw the chisel. Making a stealthy movement, he reached out. . . . Ixion, seeing victory literally within his grasp, was unsuspecting. As a feint, Jake yielded noticeably, so that the clawing hand almost touched the Webley. It was a bold move, but it paid off. Certain now that the gun was his, Ixion's mind was one-tracked. For Jake it was the moment. Raising himself on one elbow to get leverage, he swung his arm high above him and brought the chisel crashing down. The cutting edge was sharp enough yet! Ixion gave an unearthly howl as, with a sickening crunch, the chisel drove through his outstretched hand, pinning it to the floorboards.

It was only when he stood up, the gun in his hand, that Jake realised just how much his strength had ebbed. It wasn't only the grip of those hands—unbelievably strong for a man of such slight build—but the loss of blood from the wound below his shoulder. Even by the weak light of the hurricane-lamp he could see his shirt was saturated to an alarming degree. His legs felt rubbery.

As he glanced at the two moaning figures on the floor he knew he must finish them off. He gripped the gun, and pointed. But even though he remembered their cruelty, he knew he couldn't do it . . . not in cold blood. As he crossed to the window he cursed himself for a fool. Then, pocketing the gun, he took hold of the rope. . . .

He hit the water with a splash, and went under. He shot to the surface, angry with himself at forgetting that the tower on this side was bordered by the lake. Yet, what difference did it make? Shot? Drowned? It was all one. The dark water, softly lapping the castle wall, looked oily and sadistic, completing his desolation. He shivered, struck out, and reached the shore in a few strokes. The landing-lights within the castle precincts bathed the foreshore in their reflected glow, weird and shadowy. He could easily be seen : shot at.

"Nella," he called softly. "Nella, where are you?"

Twice more he called, the last time in despair. Then, casting about him, he saw . . . Could it be? Merciful God ! It was a dark shape within the shadow of the wall. His shaky legs brought him to her side. Was she alive?

She lay curled up behind the shelter of a buttress, her clothes saturated, her face white and pinched. Her arms were hugged across her breasts in an effort to warm her shivering body. His eyes went straight to that terrible hand, now stripped of its crude bandage, and he saw her thumb, scarlet and swollen. Then he saw the bullet wound; a jagged slash at the side of the neck; an awful sight. He was kneeling before her helplessly, not knowing what to do,

when her eyes opened. She looked up at him, her large
blue eyes as ebony against the ghostly oval of her face.
"J-Jake darling. . . ." She stopped, breathless, her teeth
chattering. He waited, casting a nervous look over his
shoulder. All was quiet, no one was in sight. Her lips parted
again, and in a whisper she said, "Sorry, my darling . . .
think . . . I've had it." The words, so softly uttered, seemed
to sap the last of her strength. Her eyelids drooped, and
consciousness slipped from her.

For one indecisive moment he gazed down at her, bereft
of thought; then something—her fortitude in the last few
hours, maybe—lent him strength. "All right, you bastards,
we'll show you," he muttered, raising a clenched fist in the
air. A wave of vertigo seized him as he stood up. "Must
hurry, never make it otherwise." He was talking aloud now.
The giddiness passed, but blood was seeping fast from his
shoulder as he leant over and took Nella's slim body in his
arms. With faltering footsteps, he made his way along the
edge of the lake towards the jetty. By now the helicopter's
engines had died : any minute he might hear a shot as the
castle awoke. But all remained quiet. He circled the
ramshackle hut by the landing-stage and, at the side facing
the castle, found a rickety door. He lifted the latch, and
the door opened. There was sufficient glow from the castle
lights to see the interior, and for him to pick out at the
far end a heap of sailcloth. Mouthing words of gratitude,
he crossed and laid Nella down. It made a soft enough bed,
but felt cold and damp to the touch. Coloured lights danced
before his eyes as he stood up : the giddiness was on him
again. Waiting for the attack to pass, he held on to side
of the hut. Then, on pegs near the door, he saw them :
two duffle-coats! He reached out and touched them; they
were dry enough. A bonanza find this!

He tottered outside. Must find a boat. Praise be, the
landing-lights were still on. Not a movement anywhere, but
at any moment the place could be alerted. Then it would
be pandemonium! By the landing-stage two boats were tied

up. He recognised one as the dinghy he had come over in : it had an outboard motor. Alas—useless to him : by the time he'd managed to start it, anything could happen. No, the one to take was the Pram dinghy. Nothing to do but cast off : the oars were there—on the thwarts. But, God !— if they followed in the outboard? It would only be a matter of minutes. . . . Remembering a visit to the Boat Show, he crossed to the boat and knelt down. For a moment his fingers felt for the wing nuts : they turned easily. Had he the strength to lift the outboard from the transom? Muttering words of encouragement, he got himself upright—every muscle in his back agony. A few yards along the landing-stage he dropped the outboard over the side. He watched it hit the water with a splash, roll over, and sink to the bottom.

Back in the hut, he unhooked the duffles and knelt down beside her. She looked beyond hope. Still unconscious and deathly white, she was now in the grip of an ague. That shivering body ! It needed but a glance at the sodden clothes clinging to her to know that they must come off— and at once. With trembling hands, he tore at her slacks, her jumper, her bra. . . .

It was soon done. Now she was in the duffle-coats, one round her shoulders, the other about her waist. Picking her up brought back the vertigo. Would he get to the boat? Would he manage the oars? He gritted his teeth. He got to the doorway and looked down at her face, white, drawn : utterly pathetic. "Great God." It was a sob. "She'll never make it. . . ." Then he stepped out into the pale light.

"*Don't move. Not another step.*" The words, in perfect English, were rapped out, clear and crisp.

So, at the last hurdle—after all they'd been through— he'd failed her. This was the end : there was no more fight in him.

A short, thick-set man stepped forward out of the shadows and came nearer. Jake saw the glint of a gun. The man stopped a few paces away and switched on a torch.

"Damn me," he cried, "it's Pet St Clair." The voice changed. "Who the hell are you?" he rapped.

The penny was dropping. "I'm . . . I'm Standish, Jake Standish." He could hear the voices of men, quiet voices, all around him. "You . . . you must be . . . the Commander." Then his knees were wobbling and he sank into oblivion.

Someone was rocking him up and down, gently. It was not an unpleasant sensation; something like being in a boat. Presently his eyes opened and his senses returned. High above him clouds were scurrying by. The rocking went on. Then he realised he *was* in a boat : lying in the stern. He felt like hell! He glanced down and saw he was wrapped in blankets, and his wet clothes were gone. Beside him he saw more blankets. He raised himself on one elbow. Christ! How it hurt. He looked through the gap in the blankets. It was Nella. No movement : must be dead. As he sank back, past caring, the man he knew to be the Commander walked along the jetty and looked down at him. "So you've decided to come back to us, then," he said airily.

Jake struggled to hold on to consciousness. "Is she dead? What's happened? Have I been out long?"

The Commander laughed. "Take it easy. One thing at a time, if you don't mind." In the distance Jake saw men moving : shadowy figures in the reflected light. The Commander continued : short, jerky words strung together, "Pet St Clair's tough—she'll make it. Moving off soon . . . Salzburg hospital . . . won't take long. You? . . . Been out quarter of an hour. Got castle surrounded . . . no one can escape. Good clean-up." The voice went on, "Gostoli and gang . . . arrested during night . . . well timed. . . . Good show!" Though Jake felt ghastly, the significance of the words was not lost on him.

Suddenly something galvanised the Commander into life. It was the sound of an engine starting up! "The helicopter!" he screamed.

The noise of the motors increased. Thirty seconds later they saw the helicopter rise. Above the castle wall it came, first the rotors, then the stubby fuselage. By the glare of the landing-lights they could see the pilot and another figure at his side.

The Commander roared again. "God—they've let them escape." But at that instant a shot rang out. It was a lucky hit—Jake saw the pilot pitch forward. For a moment the helicopter continued to rise, then suddenly it veered over, lost height and crashed down through the castle roof. Like the 'crump' of a million gas jets igniting, it burst into flames. Jake remembered those panelled rooms : the place would burn like tinder. A strange feeling of achievement and well-being enveloped him—for hadn't the Commander said she'd make it! He felt himself slipping. . . .

For a long time he hovered on the edge of consciousness, but when presently his eyes opened he knew the boat was almost at the other side. He took hold of the gunwale and pulled himself into a sitting position. It was a wonderful sight! Across the lake, in the pale light of dawn, the embers of the Castle of Ragensee glowed red.